the Murder of Halland

the Murder of Halland

Pia Juul

translated by Martin Aitken

Coach House Books | Toronto

First North American edition

LIBRARY AND ARCHIVES CANADA CATALOGUING IN PUBLICATION

Juul, Pia

[Mordet på Halland. English]

    The murder of Halland / Pia Juul ; Martin Aitken, translator.

Translation of: Mordet på Halland.

Translation originally published: London: Peirene Press, 2012.

ISBN 978-1-55245-314-8 (pbk)

    I. Aitken, Martin, translator II. Title. III. Title: Mordet på Halland. English.

PT8176.2.U85M6713 2015   839.813′8   C2015-905036-7

The Murder of Halland is available as an ebook: ISBN 978 1 77056 432 9

Purchase of this print book entitles you to a free digital copy. To claim your ebook of this title, please email sales@chbooks.com with proof of purchase or visit chbooks.com/digital. (Coach House reserves the right to terminate the free digital download offer at any time.)

With thanks to Herman and Gustav

May they come together,
happy in heart forever,
who long to be as one!

–Swedish Ballad (trad.)

1

The night before, we sat in the living room. I had a coffee; he drank a beer. We watched a police drama. 'I wouldn't mind looking like her,' I said, referring to the detective, Danish TV's only mature heroine. 'You don't, though, do you?' I looked over at him. Women's faces shrivel; men acquire substance. 'You've acquired substance,' I said. 'Where?' he asked, worried. 'Ha ha ha,' I laughed mockingly.

'I need to leave at seven tomorrow morning,' he said, and turned off the TV.

'I'll write for a bit.' I hugged him as tight as I could. We kissed. I rubbed my cheek against his stubble. 'Won't be long.'

In my study I tripped over something. I shuffled gingerly to the desk and turned on the lamp. My laptop was in sleep mode. Next to it stood a glass of tepid water. I swallowed a mouthful before turning to the stereo and inserting a CD. Schumann filled the room. I turned off the CD player. I can only listen to such music if the volume's turned way up, which wouldn't have pleased the neighbours at this late hour.

I switched on the laptop, picked up a book, then put it down again. I clicked open the document that came up on the screen. I had made the last set of changes two days earlier: just moved some commas, really. I thought of going to bed; perhaps he would still be awake. Feeling cold, I retrieved a sweater from the floor, pulled it over my head and began to read. Then I wrote.

Unusually, I became totally absorbed in my text and lost track of time. Eventually I looked up with an aching back. A grey dawn was breaking. I pushed the chair back and opened the window. A blackbird trilled on the roof of the summer house, greeting the loveliest of spring mornings. But when you haven't slept and your limbs feel stiff and your mind is full and empty all at once, everything seems out of sorts.

I found myself wondering how to describe the colour of the fjord. Quite unlike me, too. With the sun coming up, the water changed hue with each passing second.

I didn't want to wake Halland; he had to be up soon anyway. After going to the washroom, I went back into the living room and collapsed on the sofa under a blanket. When I opened my eyes again, I knew a sound had woken me, but I had no idea what sound. An echo reverberated inside me. I sat up and ran my fingers through my hair the way they do in films. I pulled myself together again and clutched the blanket around my knees. Was I afraid? I don't think so. That would have been psychic, insane almost. Though I remember thinking that something wasn't quite right. Had I merely heard the door closing behind Halland?

I checked the bedroom and noticed the empty bed. He had gone.

As I stood under the shower, I suddenly realized that I had seen his coat and briefcase in the hall. He hadn't left the house after all. Turning off the water, I called out to him. Nothing. The silence made me anxious. I wrapped the towel around me and moved through the house. I passed the front door and caught sight of someone through the little frosted pane. There he is, about to come in. Then the doorbell rang. 'Just a minute!' I yelled, dashing into the bedroom. I yanked off the towel and pulled on Halland's dressing gown, tying the cord as I went to open the door.

'In the name of the law!' proclaimed the bewildered-looking man on the step. His voice cracking, he raised his hand. 'It is seven forty-seven. I am arresting you for ... bear with me ...' He was out of breath.

I was stunned. Although I recognized the man, I didn't know him personally. Every morning he parked his car opposite the house, by the police station. Once I had gone to the station to get my passport renewed. I had no idea whether he was a clerk or a policeman. I didn't laugh: this clearly wasn't a laughing matter. The man was beside himself. He looked terrified.

'Are you the wife of Halland Roe?' he asked.

'I am!'

'I'm arresting you for the murder of your husband ...' Breathless, the man doubled over.

I stepped out onto the cold cobbles and looked around. A crowd had gathered at the far end of the square. Sirens approached from a distance.

'What's happened?' I asked.

Inger came out of the house next door. 'What's going on, Bjørn?' she asked the man.

'Halland Roe's been shot!' he gasped, while he gestured across the square. Then he pointed at me. '*She* did it ...'

I ran.

'Stop her!' the idiot yelled, chasing after me. But I wasn't running away; I was running to see what had happened. This was ridiculous. I was astonished not so much that I had been accused but rather that Halland was the one who had been shot. I didn't believe it. Not until I saw his body.

'If you leave me,' my ex-husband had said ten years earlier, 'you'll never see Abby again.'

'It's not for you to decide!' I replied. The shrillness in my voice surprised me. Abby was fourteen at the time; surely she could decide for herself. And she decided. Either he knew her better than I did, which was likely, or he talked her into it, which was equally possible. Since then I had only seen her a few times. She was a stubborn girl. I owned a little album with photos of her. I had looked through the pages so often that they were all dog-eared.

It is of course easy to be sentimental. She despised me; and I despised myself when I thought about it, so I hardly ever did. I nearly gave up drinking after I moved out; at least I stopped getting drunk. As I cried about Abby, I could sense through the cloud of alcohol Halland's irritation that I thought more about her than him. He didn't mind if I just drank a beer or a glass of wine as long as I remained in his thrall. He didn't need to say a thing; I knew his little signals. Anyway, if I hadn't been besotted by him, staying would have been pointless.

I stopped. I stared down at the bulk that was Halland's body. His face against the cobbles, one eye half open. His full mouth, his thin lips. His white hair combed back from his face. His black tie, his bloodstained shirt. Substance.

I thought of Abby.

The wet cobbles glistened in the morning light. Normally, the square would be deserted. Now it was filling with people. Roses bloomed against the yellow and whitewashed walls.

Someone said, 'That's her husband.' Everyone stepped back, but I had seen enough. I sensed them all staring at me. An inexplicable urge to fling myself across the body and weep overcame me, but everything seemed hazy and unreal, and theatrics wouldn't change anything. So I turned and walked back towards the house on icy feet. The door was still open. The minute I took hold of the handle, I began to shake. I staggered inside and fell to the floor, where I curled up, sobbing. But I didn't think, Halland! Oh, Halland! I thought, Abby! I want Abby!

2

Father was troubled. He narrowed his eyes. Short-sighted?
No, it was the way William Tell looked at his son under the
apple tree as he drew his crossbow and took aim.

Hugo Claus, *The Sorrow of Belgium*

I heard the commotion outside, but didn't pay any attention. I
got up and went over to the telephone on my desk. Though we
hardly ever rang each other, my mother's number was saved on
the speed dial. To warn me if she rang. She sounded surprised
to hear my voice. It was early.

'Has something happened?' she asked immediately.

I hesitated. Then I said, 'Mum, give me Abby's number. I
need to talk to her. It's important.'

'Yes, it *is* important. It's been important ever since you went
off and left her in the lurch. But why now, in the middle of
the night?'

'It's not the middle of the night! I've been up for ages!' I replied.
'Can you just give me her number?'

From the sound of the duvet shifting around her, I could
tell that she was still in bed. 'I'd prefer not to,' she said. 'I'll call
her once I'm fully awake and tell her you rang. Maybe she'll
get in touch.'

'That's not good enough!' I said desperately.

'There's something else,' she went on, suddenly sounding
more alert. 'I've been meaning to call you all week. Your grandfather wants to speak to you.'

My heart pounded; I felt the beat inside my ear.

'He wants you to go and see him.'

'Is this some kind of joke?' I asked. 'Why have you waited a week to tell me?'

'He's ill.'

We both fell silent.

'Are you still there?' she asked.

'How ill?'

'He's in hospital in Reading. He's dying.'

My breathing quickened. The doorbell rang.

'You have visitors,' said my mother.

'No, I haven't.'

'I heard the doorbell.'

'I'll call you back.' I hung up.

Grandfather. I sat staring at the telephone, at the desk with my laptop. I lifted the lid and was about to turn the laptop on when the doorbell rang again.

A tall, dark-haired man on the step said he was from the police. An old man appeared behind him. They nodded their heads, looking sombre. They wanted to come in.

'I'm not even dressed,' I said. 'And I haven't had breakfast.'

'I'll make you a nice pot of coffee while you put on some clothes,' said the tall one. 'Or perhaps you'd prefer some tea?'

I led them through the living room into the kitchen. Then I went into the bedroom and closed the door behind me. The wet towel was still on the bed. I picked it up. I sat down and pressed the speed-dial key for my mother on the wall-mounted telephone.

'That was quick,' she said.

'What's wrong with Grandfather?'

'What's not? He's ninety-six; he's got stomach cancer. He's very poorly and he wants to see you.'

'Why didn't you call me right away?'

'Who was at the door?'

'Mother, how far gone is he?'

'Are you going to go and see him or not?'

'Yes. No. I don't know. Something's happened here. Have you rung Abby?'

I caught sight of myself in the mirror. Halland's dressing gown made me look small. My wet hair was all over the place. My eyes looked strange. On the wall above the bed hung two small black-framed photographs. An unusually personal touch in this house, where my study was the only room in which I felt at home. The photos showed my grandfather and Abby. She was fourteen when I left, but here she was seven, gap-toothed and pensive, her sun-bleached summer hair tousled by a breeze. Grandfather sat in a deckchair, wearing a straw hat.

'You should go and see him,' my mother said.

'Halland's dead,' I replied, and hung up again. I rummaged through a pile of clothes on the chair until I found a pair of trousers and a top.

Someone knocked on the door. 'Come in!' I called, dragging a brush through my hair. The tall policeman stuck his head round the doorway.

'Anyone else at home besides you?' he asked.

'No. I was on the phone.'

'Who were you talking to?'

'None of your bloody business!' Then: 'If you must know, I was talking to my mother.' My voice faltered. 'I'm sorry ... It's just that ...' I buried my face in my hands. He was a stranger; I didn't want him to see me cry. 'It's just that my ...'

'Let's have that coffee,' he said.

I followed him into the living room. Somehow the place looked wrong. Still crying, I picked up the blanket from the sofa and began to fold it. The phone rang. 'Leave it,' I said. 'It's my mother. I've just spoken to her. She told me my grandfather's dying ...' I now sobbed audibly and had to sit down. 'I haven't seen him for years. And now he's dying!'

The two policemen looked at one another, then at me, then back at one another. I went into the kitchen to fetch a tissue.

'You do realize why we're here?' said the older man.

I nodded imperceptibly. 'I saw him in the square.'

'Halland Roe has been shot. He's dead. Are you Bess?'

I nodded again.

'His wife?'

'We're not married,' I said, gazing around the room. 'We've lived together for ten years. This is Halland's house. Do you want to arrest me again?'

'Arrest you?'

'A man came ... Bjørn. He said I shot Halland.'

'Did you?'

Tears welled up once more. I didn't answer. Instead, I wept for my grandfather and for Halland and for Abby, and for all my silly attempts at being purposeful. Just a moment ago, the desire to speak to Abby had seemed so obvious, as though nothing else mattered. Now I didn't know any longer what I wanted.

A gunshot had woken me. That's what the noise had been. Bjørn worked as the caretaker at the school on the other side of the square; he had seen Halland stagger and then fall. And he believed he had heard Halland say, 'My wife has shot me.'

Gazing at me with pity, the policemen spoke, but I didn't understand a word. I didn't grasp that they wanted an explanation. The thought that I was somehow involved didn't occur to me. I didn't realize that they were trying to find out whether I could have shot Halland. They didn't actually say as much, so I'm just guessing. But obviously they were waiting for me to say something. What I eventually said was, 'Can I see him again?'

I could, but later.

I stopped crying and sipped my coffee. The policeman had used the French press. It would have been dusty, but hopefully he had bothered to rinse it. I noticed that the dark-haired cop was talking to me and I looked up.

'What was your name again?' I asked.

'Detective Funder.'

'Funder,' I repeated.

'Does Halland have any family? Brothers or sisters? Children, perhaps?'

'No …' I replied, then paused. 'As far as I know, his family are all dead. He'd lost touch with his sister by the time she died.'

'Was Halland married before you and he got together?'

'No. Why do you want to know?'

Funder looked disappointed.

'He can't possibly have said his wife shot him. What exactly did he say? Could Bjørn have misheard? How come he didn't see what happened?'

'Halland was shot with a hunting rifle.'

'How do you know?'

'From the sound of the gunshot and from the entry wound. The shot was fired from some distance away. Bjørn didn't see the gunman, and Halland won't have seen anyone either.'

'Then why did Bjørn say what he said?'

'Why, indeed,' said Funder. 'Do you or Halland own a hunting rifle?'

No. We didn't own any weapons.

No, I didn't shoot Halland.

No, I hadn't seen him since last night.

No, I had no idea why anyone would want to kill him.

And no, Halland had no enemies. Enemies only existed in films. As indeed did being shot. Anyway, what did I know about Halland's life outside of this house?

'*And wouldst thou be free of sadness and sorrow, thou shouldst love nought upon this Earth,*' I mused.

The police officers looked up quizzically.

'Ludvig Bødtcher.' I said.

3

Two feelings at odds within me, I can still remember that much;
my memory's best when it comes to contradictory feelings.

Christa Wolf, *In the Flesh*

They wanted to see the car so I fetched my key from the hook in the kitchen. As we passed through the hall, I pointed at Halland's coat and briefcase. They checked the coat pockets. Then they opened the briefcase, looked inside and closed it again.

There was nothing in the car. Just an empty plastic box that stayed in the trunk, Halland's wellies, his bird book, a torch and a small pair of binoculars.

'He hasn't been near the car today,' I said. I didn't know if that was true, but it sounded right.

After the policemen left, I lay down on the living-room floor. There was no space anywhere else. The furniture seemed all wrong. I lay there waiting, emptied out. I didn't dare to think, but my thoughts were racing. Then it was quiet again. I felt sick and sleepy. I stared into space. I noticed cobwebs on the ceiling but I didn't get up to remove them. Then I wanted to find a photograph of Halland as a child. I knew we had some. I remembered one of him on holiday with a calf in his arms. He had called the animal a 'maverick' when he showed me the picture. I wondered where the photograph could be. It wasn't in any of the albums. Where were Halland's hiding places? How come I had even seen that photograph? I tried to visualize him holding it in his hand. I lost myself in the memory: the dinner table, the guests, the photo, laughter. Breakfast in the kitchen, newspaper, coffee, long hair: a dream retold – and the photograph. What had he dreamt? Did I listen?

The policemen returned a few hours later to collect me. On the way out of town, I heard a skylark through the open window. Its song filled me with sudden joy, then with abrupt dismay because of the joy. I said nothing. The others sat in silence too.

Halland lay alone in a bare room with a sheet over him. He looked the same and yet he didn't. I both knew him and didn't know him. I was his and he was mine, only now we weren't. We were both alone. I laid my hand gently against his cheek, a gesture I made whenever he seemed in pain and I didn't have the courage to ask him if anything was wrong.

'Halland,' I whispered. 'Maverick!' I had never said that word out loud in my life. Why did I say it now? With his smooth skin, Halland resembled a dead Indian chief deprived of his feathers. I pressed my lips to his forehead. It wasn't a kiss. I just didn't have the heart not to touch him.

Funder ushered me into a space, half office, half waiting room. 'Don't worry,' he said, 'we'll drive you home soon. But I want to ask you some questions first. Did Halland have a cell phone?'

'Yes. A blue one.' I felt cold.

'Do you know where it is?'

'In his shirt pocket? If it's not in his jacket or his briefcase, I wouldn't know. I can look …'

'Let us know if it turns up. We'll be coming round later anyway. Then there's his keys …' He put them on the table: Halland's car keys on a keyring – a miniature Eiffel Tower – and the keys to the house. There was a third, unfamiliar set too: one ordinary-looking key and another for a security lock. 'Do you know what these are for?'

Pointing at the third set, I said, 'I've never seen those before. Where did you find them?'

'In his trouser pocket. We found this too.' A little wallet with a clip. Inside Halland kept his driving licence and his debit card. 'Were the keys to do with his work, perhaps?'

'He works from home.'

'Do you have a holiday home or an apartment somewhere?'

I had no idea where the two keys came from. Besides, I felt exhausted and past caring. Funder took me home. In the car I was about to nod off, but he was keen to give me some advice. 'The news has already been announced on the radio, so there'll be journalists,' he said. 'You don't need to speak to them.'

I had no intention of speaking to them. Funder said I shouldn't be alone.

'I like being on my own; I'm used to it. Halland's away so much, and I've no one to ...' Then, lying, I said I'd ask Inger to come round.

'Halland is dead; he's been murdered. You'll be feeling vulnerable. In fact you don't know how you're going to feel. Not yet.'

'Neither do you! I'd prefer to be on my own. I don't like ... people.'

A TV-news unit was parked at the far end of the square when he dropped me off. I ignored them and hurried into the house where I turned on my laptop.

Thirty-seven new messages. The subject line 'My beloved husband' caught my eye. When I opened the email, the line expanded to 'My beloved husband – characters'. The message concerned one of my stories: 'I'm in the process of analyzing your short story "My Beloved Husband," which, incidentally, is extremely well written. I'm sure you must be very busy with other matters, but I wonder whether you could find the time to send me some information about each of the characters. Thanks in advance.'

'Busy with other matters' indeed. I opened the next message.

'I have just read your short story "The Fjord." I'm writing an essay comparing it to other works. I wonder if you might say something about the story's background? I can analyze it from the outside, but the views of the author would be very helpful. You have probably got more important things to do, so I will understand completely if you don't reply.'

Normally, I would find such emails touching. I always replied to them, so I dealt with the two queries straight away, copying a couple of old responses rather than writing from scratch. But suddenly I stopped and rested my hands in my lap and closed my eyes. In many of my public readings I had been struck by disturbing thoughts. What if Halland fell ill or died? What if I broke my leg? What if Abby turned up? I always tried to weigh up probabilities. At what point would I cancel an engagement? Now my husband was dead and here I was replying to meaningless emails. I deleted both of my replies, aware that they could be retrieved, and moved on to the ones with the subject line 'HALLAND.' There were several. From my cousin, my publisher, colleagues, even distant acquaintances. Filled with shock and compassion. I merely scanned the words but realized that everyone sensed the gravity of the situation more keenly and more immediately than I had. But why had no one called? I picked up the phone. Dead. I replaced the receiver tried again, but there was no dial tone. Shivering, I wondered what to do next. I pulled the phone lead towards me and saw the plug lying loose on the floor. Where was my cell phone? I ought to call someone and tell them what had happened. But I couldn't think who. There was an email with the subject line 'REMINDER.' I was supposed to give a talk at a library in Jutland in a fortnight's time. They were sending me instructions about how to get there. Had they heard the news on the radio? Did they know my husband had been shot? No. I had no intention of replying to them. Should I create an auto reply saying my husband had been murdered?

I turned off the laptop. The house was quiet. I had sat here writing last night. What had I written? I didn't want to think about my work. Perhaps I would never want to think about writing again. That belonged to the past and didn't matter any longer. I looked out at the fjord. The sun glittered on the water.

4

Everyone avoids seeing a man born, everyone runs to see him die.

Montaigne, *Essays*

The hospital in Reading showed no interest in helping me find my grandfather. As I waited to be passed from one voice to the next, I wondered whether I could travel to England and back on the same day. It seemed possible. Though Halland was dead, I didn't see how flying to London would be a problem. I tried to visualize my grandfather. Had he grown smaller as old people do, especially sick ones? Did he have the wild look in his eyes that I had seen in people who would die shortly afterwards? Would I be able to embrace him? Would he recognize me? Would he have the strength to admonish me, or would he forgive me? Why did he want to see me? Because he was dying. But for my sake or for his? I didn't have the courage to visit him.

'I've spoken to Julian and he would like to talk to you,' said a nurse. 'We can wheel a phone over to his bed. I'll give you the number and you can call him in ten minutes.'

I half got up to call for Halland, then sat down again, embarrassed. I closed my eyes for a moment. My cousin had married when I was still in my teens. I had been deeply impressed by the wedding, and especially my grandfather's speech. 'Never let the sun set on your anger,' he told the happy couple. What lovely advice, I thought, and decided that I would follow it when I got married. My mother, though, went off the deep end about my grandfather's speech: 'He could go for days without saying a word to Mum, all because of some little thing that annoyed him. No wonder she died before her time!' My grandfather had shunned me for ten years. Maybe because of Abby, maybe because he opposed divorce. I didn't know. He behaved wonderfully towards me during my childhood. Now he wouldn't answer my letters. After the separation, I had attended a couple of family get-togethers. When I sat down next to him, he got up and went to the other end of the room. I didn't care about the family if Abby wasn't there. And most of them didn't want to see me anyway; they wanted to see her. In the end, they kept their distance and I kept mine.

I deliberately didn't plan what to say before I rang the hospital back. My grandfather didn't sound poorly or even especially weak. 'Hello?' he barked.

'Grandfather, it's Bess. Mum said you wanted to talk to me?'

'Yes. I'd prefer to see you face to face.'

'I would like to visit, but something's happened ... Halland ... my husband. How are you?'

'Not well, my dear.'

'One of the photographs hanging on the wall above my bed shows you sitting in a deckchair wearing a straw hat. Do you remember? I look at it every night before I go to sleep.'

'I've been foolish, my dear,' he said. He never called me 'my dear' when I was a girl. 'We're all so fond of Abby. I suppose that's why we didn't ...'

Now he did sound poorly.

'I'm very happy we're speaking now,' I said.

'I'm a great-great-grandfather! Did you know?'

'Yes! I've seen baby Sofie!'

'Do you know ...' – he winced, or shifted his weight – 'who was there when she was born?'

I did know: my cousin's daughter – the baby's mother – her husband, her mother and her sister.

'Three witnesses,' he spluttered, 'and here I am, all on my own! You all live so far away. What a mess!'

'Grandfather, I'll come and see you as soon as I can.'

'All right, dear, all right,' he said. 'Bye.'

A commotion followed as though he had dropped the receiver. I continued to listen. The line was still connected, but no one said anything. All I could hear was a hiss and what sounded like footsteps in a corridor. I hung up. I didn't cry, only stared at the phone. After a while I looked out of the window at the fjord. Was that all?

I thought of calling Halland. And remembered I couldn't. Then again, perhaps I could. Where was his cell phone? I could make it ring somewhere. In a bush. In a car. In the pocket of a stranger, a man with a hunting rifle. I pressed 1. The number didn't pick up.

Now I could only wait for Abby to call. Perhaps I should call my mother again, but I didn't want to speak to her. The police would be coming back. But what about Halland? I went into the hall to check on his briefcase. It was still standing in the same spot and his coat still hung on the same peg. Why had he left the house without his coat and briefcase? His big binoculars stood on the windowsill in the living room, so he hadn't gone out because he had seen a bird. No one had rung the doorbell; I would have heard that. I rummaged in his pockets, even though I had seen the police checking them earlier. They were empty. I picked up the briefcase and went upstairs.

This was Halland's domain – a place I hardly ever entered. Here was his office. Next door was the guest room. At the far end was empty loft space with a clothes line and some junk.

I felt apprehensive as I pushed open the door to his office. I am just putting the briefcase away, I told myself. I went over to the window, looked out. How tidy his desk was! A bulldog clip holding receipts, two ballpoint pens, a calendar. That was it.

On the wall above the desk hung a black-and-white photograph. I took the picture down and wiped the dust off the glass with my sleeve. It showed Halland and me on our way to a film premiere. A press photographer had caught the moment. Not that we posed; we just happened to be snapped on our way past. I could see why Halland had hung up the picture. It was our first year together and we were happy. Anyone could see that. At least I could, now. Halland's hair had turned completely white during his illness, but here his long mane was dark and only just starting to turn grey. I traced the sharp line of his nose with my finger, his full mouth. He was looking at me, saying something. What did we say to each other in those days? What did we ever say? I couldn't remember us talking. Did we even say good morning? Yes, we said good morning.

5

Why did you call me 'Deer of Heaven'? It makes no sense. It sounded beautiful then, but it was childish.

Friedrich Glauser, *Thumbprint*

That night in the hotel, I got out of bed and stood at the window smoking. I gazed across the square into an illuminated apartment occupied by people leading ordinary lives. I came to a decision which I then found myself unable to carry out. The act of making a decision can propel you along for a while, even if you never do anything. I wore my jacket to keep out the chill. Turning away from the window, I let the jacket fall to the floor. I felt my way around the bed to the armchair where I had left my clothes. Light from the street lamp fell across his naked, snoring bulk sprawled diagonally across the bed. I put on my clothes, retrieved my jacket and shoulder bag and tiptoed away.

That was the night I left him ten years ago. That was also the night I returned without him realizing I had been gone. He was lying as I had left him, drunk as a lord.

The next day we went to the seaside. For hours we strolled along the beach, lay in the sand and dozed. Later we had dinner outdoors, generous helpings of shellfish and chilled wine. We sat under a lean-to in the evening light, waves lapping, conversation subdued and desultory, until we had run out of words. We sat at the back of the bus as we jolted our way to the hotel. We didn't speak. Finally, I laid my head in his lap and wept silently. He stroked my hair. 'I know why you're crying.'

This tender comment, however uncharacteristic of him, was one of the reasons I decided to stay. Even though I knew very well that he couldn't have guessed why I wept. He didn't know that I had tried to leave him. He didn't know that I cried because I had failed. And he certainly didn't know that I missed my daughter. Yet the tenderness in his voice soothed me and I cherished the moment as though it had already turned into a fond memory. Had he not said what he said, I would never have thought of him as the love of my life. I never asked him if he understood my real feelings. I never asked him anything.

We never grew closer than on that night. In the silence. In the darkness as we dined. In the harsh light of the bus. In his touch and in the tenderness of his voice.

6

He was killed by an exploding television set – unorthodox to the last.

Preben Geertinger, *Confessions of a Pathologist*

I saw 'lust' where the text said 'last.' I tried to continue reading, but couldn't. I mused on my mistake, marvelling at the ability to read in the first place. How did the eyes work? And the brain? Just as I wobbled on a bike if I allowed myself to think about balance, my reading became shaky if I wondered about the mechanism of reading. I loved reading and had always thought of it as a refuge. I even read the labels on bottles, if only to keep myself occupied on trains or in restaurants. I read in bed at night. If I lay awake for more than two minutes after switching off the light, I switched it on again to avoid lapsing into thought. To avoid thinking.

I gained this understanding the morning after Halland's murder. I had managed an hour or so of sleep on the sofa. I tried to watch a film, to find something to read. I scanned the spine of every volume I owned without finding anything suitable. All the books I had bought just for their titles and which I had never read. Time was too short. *The Far Islands and Other Cold Places. Travel Essays of a Victorian Lady.* I resolved to read the latter in due course. I waited for Abby to call, knowing that she wouldn't. Eventually, I settled on a book, only because its size fitted into my back pocket. I put on a sweater, covered my head with a scarf and went out with a newspaper tucked under my arm. It was five o'clock in the morning. The light was grey, the grass was wet. The summer house was cold and damp. I walked down to the shore. The sun wouldn't come out today; I could feel it in my bones. I sensed some movement behind me but didn't dare turn round. Was someone watching me? All of a sudden, my legs threatened to give way.

I lay the newspaper on the jetty, sat down and opened my book. Again I thought about my obsession with reading and smiled to myself. 'Lust' instead of 'last.' I stared at the fjord's leaden waters and realized my vulnerability. I had sat reading on the jetty on other occasions; I was a writer after all. Halland always maintained that writers were privileged creatures. The more foolish and bizarre their behaviour, the happier they made those around them. Partly because other people's prejudices were confirmed, partly because such conduct inspired outrage. Halland had lectured me on the subject, insisting that anyone who made a spectacle of herself couldn't really blame others for doing the same. But he could hardly have been thinking of a situation like this. Someone sitting on a jetty at five thirty in the morning would barely be noticed. But if her husband had just been murdered? The situation could so easily be misconstrued. A grieving woman could sit alone on a jetty in the early morning. But not with a book in her hands.

I put the book back in my pocket. The jetty creaked. I was resting my chin on my knees when I saw a figure approaching out of the corner of my eye.

In the past – though now I found the obsession ridiculous, even disturbing – I had likened strangling to a caress but considered shooting as callous. I had wanted to write a story about the difference between them. Now I was unable to fathom my excitement about intimate forms of murder (passion/strangulation) as opposed to calculated, remote forms of murder (callousness/shooting). Murder was murder, I thought, as the figure approached. I was overcome by a feeling of nausea. I imagined hands closing around my throat. Someone was aiming a rifle at me from further up the hill.

A man stopped beside me. I didn't know him. 'Morning,' he said, then continued the last few metres to the end of the jetty, where wooden steps led down to the water. I nodded wordlessly. He filled a pipe with tobacco and then struck a match. The smoke wrapped itself around me. Its fragrance was sweet. The sun broke through the clouds. I stood up.

'Lovely, isn't it?' he said.

'Yes,' I replied, and looked out over the fjord to see if I agreed. He sat down. As I was turning away, he said something else. All I heard was 'Halland.'

'I beg your pardon?' I said.

'I'm sorry about Halland.'

'Thank you,' I replied, walking off briskly. I didn't care who he was, or how he knew me. I could see the white-painted summer house with the silly weathervane. A blackbird sang. I went up the path. It could have been a normal day. I could have been going back to make coffee and wake Halland. When I reached the garden, I stopped and looked back on the jetty. The man hadn't moved. If he was a journalist, he certainly wasn't the keen sort. The smoke from his pipe created a cloud around him. I had forgotten my newspaper; it stuck to the wet planks. The fjord lay calm. Its bluish-grey surface glistened here and there with the rays of the sun. I almost didn't feel sorry.

7

Christian VI had no mistresses and waged no wars.
A Concise History of Denmark

Caution in the face of novelty. The hesitant curiosity I had felt about Halland, about the house in which we were going to live, about the garden. The place was ours, yet I held back. I experienced the world with provisos.

The call of a cuckoo startled me. Cuckoos were supposed to call from far off, not from a tree in one's own garden. What did they say about the cuckoo's call, about death and how many years you had left? But death had already come and gone. Or was the cuckoo calling for me? I shied away from trying to understand Halland's death. Out of fear? But I was not afraid. And now my grandfather was about to die as well. For many years I had missed him terribly; now I didn't want to see him. I felt nothing any more, not sorrow, not grief.

I went back upstairs to Halland's office. I stood for a moment, then sat down in his chair, closed my eyes and inhaled deeply. The room smelled of nothing in particular, dust perhaps, the warm fragrance of wood from the furniture. Under the desk was a pair of roll-front cabinets, one to the left, one to the right. The keys were in the locks. When I opened the one on the left, the roll-front clattered to the floor. The drawers were nearly empty: some letters and a couple of brochures, a few loose photographs of the garden and the view out over the fjord, some of me, one of Halland's mother. I didn't find the photo with the maverick.

The drawers of the right-hand cabinet were full of documents to do with Halland's business: VAT forms, tax forms, old mileage records. Although I had never rummaged through his papers, I didn't feel I was intruding. Halland's tidiness made me feel safe. Then I saw the two keys, this time on a loop of string: an ordinary one and one for a security lock. Halland had tied a little tag to them: SPARES. They looked exactly like the ones Funder had shown me. I weighed them in my hand before returning them to the drawer. Then I pulled up the roll-front and rose to my feet. Next, I opened the cabinet again, pulled out the drawer, took the keys and put them in my pocket. Leaving the cabinet unlocked, I went downstairs, only to change my mind again. I returned to Halland's office, removed the cabinet drawers one by one and searched through their contents. I didn't know what I was looking for. A piece of paper, perhaps, with the words THIS IS WHAT THE KEYS ARE FOR. Anyway, I found nothing.

I slumped over the desk and rested my head on my arms for what seemed like a long time, my nose pressed into the fragrant wood.

Funder had left a card with his number. I could call him. On the other hand, I expected the police to return. Weren't they supposed to pursue their inquiries? Shouldn't they be going through Halland's things, questioning me, making progress on the case? Somewhere out there was a man with a hunting rifle – and he had to be found. But they would hardly find him here. I had discovered some keys. The police already had a set. So I didn't call Funder.

I had to get out. Go for a walk or do some shopping. Anything. As I left the house, a figure ducked behind an open door. Then the door slammed shut as if someone had kicked it. Were people avoiding me?

Despite the sunshine, a chill lingered in the air. On the high street outside the newsagents I recognized Halland's shadowy face on a tabloid placard. WHO SHOT HALLAND? asked the headline. Where did they find that photo? As so often, anger grabbed me and I was about to storm into the newsagents. Hadn't Halland been a customer for years? Where were their manners? Did they even know what manners were? However, I turned on my heel and took a short cut down to the stream. My breathing quietened. My mind ran on two parallel tracks: one thinking about nothing, merely existing, the other churning out unpleasant explanations. At least I managed to hold the second track at bay. I clasped the unfamiliar keys in my pocket as I criss-crossed the narrow streets. Suddenly I heard a car behind me. This is it, I thought. Now they are going to run me over. What will death feel like? Will I scream or fall silently? But nothing happened.

8

Being there for each other in the proper way is a fine art.
Peter Seeberg, *Shepherds*

Inger came outside just as I was unlocking my front door. 'I don't
know what to say,' she said.

'I know.'

'Is he really dead?'

'It says so in the paper.'

'Was he really shot?'

'Didn't you hear the shot?' I asked, vaguely interested in what
she would say.

'Yes, I did. The sound woke me up. At first, I thought it was
Lasse coming home late. Have they found the murderer?'

I didn't reply.

'How are you doing?'

I didn't reply.

'It always happens to the person next door, doesn't it?' she said.
'But I don't want it to happen to the person next door. I'm frightened. Aren't you frightened?'

She always had something to say; she was constantly jabber-
ing on. I cocked my hip, the posture I used to adopt as a bored
teenager. I had never stood that way since. I was fond of Inger,
but I didn't want to listen to her.

'On the inside I'm the same person I've always been,' she went
on. 'I look at myself in the mirror in the mornings and think,
It's high time you had an early night. Then I think, But you had

an early night *last* night, *and* the night before. It's just the way I look! Shocks me every morning because I feel young inside, or at least the same as I've always felt.'

I didn't think Inger looked old, but then I myself didn't feel like the same person inside any more. Perhaps she was expecting me to say something. I couldn't.

'Where have you been?' she asked.

'Shopping.'

'Are you hungry?'

'No.'

'I'll leave a casserole on the step for your supper. You might want something by then.'

I went inside. The postman had come. When I picked up the newspaper and a letter, I recognized my mother's handwriting and tore open the envelope. The phone rang. As I dashed into the bedroom to answer it I banged my leg against the bed frame. Rubbing my knee, I picked up the receiver, expecting to hear Abby's voice. It was a journalist. I pulled the plug out of the wall. The letter lay crumpled in my hand. It read: 'Dear Bess. She doesn't want to. I've told her you called and that Halland is dead, but she doesn't want to. What did he die of? Love, Mum.' Why didn't she call to tell me? Was this her idea of a condolence letter?

I had led a good life with Abby and her father. A normal, everyday life full of joy, sex, laughter, boredom, drudgery, acrimony and minor arguments. My husband took a sabbatical from his teaching job to go on some courses. He travelled a lot that year. I met Halland. If the five-minute encounter in a bookshop could have been avoided, everything would have worked out differently. Of course, any event can be thought of as inevitable or as something you could have altered or ignored.

The moment I told him I was leaving, my husband became consumed by a fury I never knew he had in him. For a year, Halland and I tried, though never consciously, to make my decision to live with him work. We really tried. We went on holiday and to parties. During the summer, we swam in the fjord every morning. Had people round. Planted roses. I painted the little summer house white; we put a weathervane on the roof. We never had any children, though. Before the year was out, Abby's father became the father of twins. There was no turning back. A cliché, for sure. But it described reality. Abby wouldn't see me. Halland and I were happy – at least until he fell ill.

Despite our year together we barely knew each other, and our relationship became more difficult as his condition worsened. Though we ate together and shared a bed, I felt as shy and awkward as I had been when we first met. That never changed. Right from the beginning I kept my sanitary towels, make-up, lotions, even my vitamin pills hidden away in drawers in my study. I rarely revealed myself to Halland, not if I had time to think before I spoke. The thoughts sounded wrong inside my head so they never came out of my mouth. Eventually I convinced myself that we understood one another without recourse to words. His personal belongings and affairs were so inconspicuous that I never considered them at all. But his illness filled my entire consciousness. I couldn't look away any longer. I helped him in little ways, though I spoke of the illness as seldom as possible. Only once did I ask him if he was in pain. He turned away without replying, because he *was* in pain, I suppose, but I never knew. Poor Halland. I think he would have liked to have known me.

I stood in the living room. The lid of the piano was open. Halland had put candles in the holders. He had given me the piano when I moved in with him because I had told him I played. The only time I showed any interest in the instrument was the day the tuner came. I still had 'Golliwog's Cakewalk' at my fingertips. Part of it, anyway. But then I ground to a halt and didn't return to the keyboard other than to run a duster over it, which happened rarely. We never spoke about the piano again. Now I began rummaging for my childhood sheet music. I found the box and placed it on the coffee table. I sorted through the sheets, chose a piece and began to play. Progress was slow, but I was in no hurry. When I looked up, I realized that an hour had passed. I felt at peace.

I had left a window open onto the street. A man stood in the square as if listening. At first he didn't bother me, until I recognized him as the man from the jetty. What on earth was he doing here? I noisily closed the window. He acknowledged me with a nod and went on his way.

9

The monkey looked the buzzard right dead in the eye and said,
'Your story's so touching, but it sounds jes' like a lie.'
Irving Mills, *Straighten Up and Fly Right*

I waited until dusk before going to see whether Inger had left supper on the step. I had already decided to bin the food, but as I carried the casserole into the kitchen, my stomach suddenly knotted. I couldn't remember if I had eaten since Halland's death. The smell of the cold stew wafted out as I lifted the dripping lid. I grabbed a fork and ate straight from the pot, standing up at the kitchen counter. My stomach contracted. I left the fork in the pot, guzzled some water from the tap and then threw myself onto the sofa, burying my face in the cushions and drawing the blanket over me. I closed my eyes and kicked off my shoes. I felt sated and drowsy, serene and utterly relaxed. Now I could sleep. But my mouth filled with acid. I knew what that meant, the familiar twinge behind my eyes. When I swallowed, the bile rose again, more insistent. My head began to spin. I flung the blanket aside and raced into the hall, reaching the toilet just as Inger's stew flew out of my mouth in a cascade of vomit. I slumped groaning on the bathroom floor. 'Ugh!' The sound helped. The floor was warm. I lay there for a moment – the briefest of moments – curled into a ball till the doorbell rang. It was dark outside. My body ached. The floor was hard, and I had no idea how long I had slept.

Someone stood in the light of the street lamp, but I couldn't see who. As I opened the door my queasiness faded. The young woman wasn't Abby. Doe-eyed, legs apart, a duffel bag over her shoulder, she seemed to be thrusting her pregnant stomach right at me.

'Sorry to turn up so late,' she said, not sounding at all apologetic. 'It's such a chore getting here from Copenhagen without a car. The journey took longer than I expected.'

'Who are you?'

'I'm Pernille.'

'Have we met?'

'I'm Halland's niece. I read about his death in the paper. Didn't he ever mention me?'

I stood aside so she could come in. The fact that Halland had a niece was news to me. Dropping her bag on the floor in the hall, she looked around.

'Well!' she exclaimed. 'So this is Uncle Halland's little love nest ...' She now stood in the living room, nostrils quivering. A doe indeed.

'This is where he lived,' I said, 'and for a good many years as well. I don't recall him ever mentioning you. Are you Hanne's daughter? I didn't think she had any children.'

'No,' Pernille replied.

'Would you like something to drink?' I asked, gesturing towards the sofa in case she wanted to sit down.

'Water would be fine,' she said.

I went into the kitchen. As I turned on the tap, I had a brainwave.

'You're Hanne's foster-child,' I said, handing Pernille a glass of water.

She nodded. 'My parents are dead. When Hanne died, Halland was the only family I had left.'

'Was he indeed?' I felt dizzy and sat down. 'Were you thinking of staying here?'

Pernille didn't reply.

'Do you *want* to stay here?'

She nodded.

'Listen,' I went on, 'I need to go to bed. Can we talk in the morning?'

'I'm tired as well,' she said. 'But can't we talk now?'

'What about?' I sensed unpleasant news coming my way. 'Perhaps I'd better make some coffee.'

'You're a writer, aren't you?' Pernille asked as I filled the espresso maker. 'What are you working on?'

'What do you mean, what am I *working on*?' I glared at her from the doorway. 'Don't try to have a normal conversation with me! Halland is dead! Isn't that why you're here? Or was there something else?'

She began to cry. Even in floods of tears she looked adorable. I turned on the gas. My hands were shaking because I had shouted the word *dead*. Only a simple word. But I shook because the word described the truth. Halland was *dead*.

What did Pernille want? I grabbed a piece of crispbread from the cupboard and gnawed it as I went back into the living room.

'Why are you here? Does your husband know where you are?'

Startled, she looked up. 'I haven't got a husband,' she said, passing her hand across her stomach. 'Halland was the only family I had left. I was so shocked to read about what happened.' She wiped her eyes.

'He's not your family!' I said, rather too emphatically.

'No, but he keeps his things ...'

'What things?'

'The things in his room.'

His room.

You're lying, a voice said inside me. I don't know why, but you're lying, you're lying, you're lying. I didn't accuse her to her face though. I simply gazed at her brown eyes, her nose, her swollen stomach.

'He's been paying rent, and now I don't know what to do. About the rent, I mean. His things can stay where they are for the time being.'

The rent.

'And then there's … well, I suppose this sounds odd, but he promised he'd be with me when the baby came.' She glanced over at me, her mouth slightly open, showing her white teeth.

Looking up at the ceiling, I stifled a sneer. Halland and hospitals … Did she have any idea what she was talking about? And did I want to know if she did?

'I could do without this,' I said. My words surprised me, because I was actually curious. Nevertheless I was determined not to know more. Not yet. Tomorrow, perhaps. Pernille had come to me with a problem she wanted me to solve, not realizing that she created one for me in the process.

'We can talk about the rent in the morning,' I said. 'I need to get some sleep.'

I took Pernille up to the guest room. On the way back downstairs, I realized how much I wanted to sleep in my own bed. I splashed cold water on my face and took off my clothes, threw them in the washing basket and went into the bedroom. I switched on my reading lamp and climbed in under the covers. There I lay, gazing at where Halland was supposed to be. I reached out to touch him. I closed my eyes. They were burning. I was exhausted. I switched off the lamp and found myself migrating to his side of the bed, crawling under his duvet, inhaling his scent as deeply as I could, embracing his pillow, burying my face deeper and deeper. 'Halland,' I breathed. And again, louder this time. To no avail.

10

The landscape is of no consequence to us. We are not poets;
our delight is in consistent activity.

Peter Seeberg, *The Spy*

I awoke to the sound of rain falling, saw light coming through
the window and felt relieved. With no dreams to digest, I simply
listened and savoured the peace.

The next moment something was wrong. After my divorce I
used to wake in the mornings heavy with grief, as if someone
had died. But when I saw Halland lying next to me, I realized
no one had died. He was there. But Abby was gone. Now I
turned and saw my empty side of the bed. I lay on Halland's
side. He was dead. And a pregnant woman was sleeping in the
bedroom upstairs.

The last night we spent here together, I slept well until I
awoke suddenly. The room was dark and silent. I switched on
the lamp and checked the clock.

'What's the time?' he asked.

'Half past three. Why are we awake?'

But he was already asleep again. A night like any other, with
a waking moment.

'It's raining outside!' Penille announced when she finally
came tripping into the kitchen, looking for breakfast.

'Where else would it be raining?' I slammed the bread basket
down on the table. She was about to laugh but caught herself
when she saw my expression.

45

'There's crispbread and toast, and no milk for your coffee,'
I said. 'I haven't done any shopping. There's been a death in
the family.'

Turning back to the cooker, I listened for sniffling sounds.
There they were. Good.

'I'll run you to the station,' I said, sitting down at the table.
'I can't have you here. You're taking my grief away.' I actually
said that.

'You don't seem very sad.'

'That's exactly what I mean! I won't have you sitting here wailing – I'm the one who's lost him, not you!'

'I have too!' How hurt she looked.

I crunched furiously on some crispbread until I realized that
something was wrong. I spat the whole lot out in my hand,
crispbread and spit and half a molar. 'Oh no,' I cried. 'Who do
you think you are anyway, coming here?'

'I'll get my things,' she said quietly, and disappeared.

I stared at the fragment of tooth. My tongue probed the
empty space. My eyes filled with tears.

I was on my way out to the car when I saw Funder coming
towards me. He held a folded newspaper over his head as
though that would prevent him from getting wet.

'I was just going out,' I said, trying to draw his attention away
from Pernille.

'I need to look through Halland's belongings. His desk, his
computer.'

I darted back to the house and inserted my key in the lock,
picturing Halland's empty desk. Where was his laptop?

'I've got a spare house key in the car. Halland's office is
upstairs. Please don't disturb my papers. I know it looks a mess,
but there's a system ...'

Funder nodded, scrutinizing me closely. I talked too fast. I wanted to avoid getting wet but that didn't explain my odd behaviour. I reached into my pocket and wrapped my hand around Halland's mysterious keys.

'Just pop the house key through the letter box when you're finished,' I said.

'Don't you want an update on our progress?'

'Must I?' Was I actually flirting? Couldn't I give the policeman a straight answer? Why did Funder have such a deep tan in the middle of May? He smiled. The rain dripped slowly from his hair. Did I look like someone in mourning? Was I mourning? I didn't really care what he thought. No, actually, I did.

I only returned to the car after he had gone inside and shut the door behind him. Pernille, holding an umbrella, stood impatiently next to the car.

'If you miss the train, there'll be another one in an hour,' I told her. Reversing the car, I added, 'So, tell me about this room.' Another car approached. I waited then backed out and turned.

'Didn't you know?'

'Know what?' The engine stalled. Inhaling deeply, I turned the key in the ignition. Wipers on. Concentrate.

'Why have you stopped?' Pernille asked.

'I haven't stopped.' I swerved to avoid a cyclist. Concentrate. Leave the gears alone. Down the hill to the main road.

'You've got a licence, haven't you?' she asked.

The rain pelted down now.

'Do you have a key to Halland's room?' I asked.

'No.'

'But it's locked?'

'Yes. Sometimes he leaves his laptop there and, well – he locks the door after him.'

'How often is he there?'

'Don't you know?'

I didn't reply.

'He stopped by a fortnight ago and was supposed to come yesterday. I didn't always know in advance. He'd let himself in.'

'I'll come and clear it out as soon as I can.'

'It's more the rent, really …'

'I'll keep up the payments as long as his things are there. It'll be a while before I can get into town. I'll need the address …'

Pernille took a scrap of paper from her bag, wrote something and then propped the paper up on the dashboard, saying, 'My number's there, too.' Turning away, she gazed out of the side window. My tongue examined the crater that my molar had left.

'What about the birth?' she asked.

'That's enough! What is it with you? Can't women give birth any more without the whole family looking on?'

She didn't reply. We had left the town behind us and picked up speed. The road was empty.

'Do you seriously think I'd want to be there in Halland's place and watch you give birth?'

'No.'

'When's it due?'

'Two months.'

'Isn't there someone else you can ask? A girlfriend, perhaps?'

Surely a doe-eyed beauty would have lots of friends. Pernille didn't reply. Perhaps she was crying; I couldn't tell. I wondered where to drop her off. Not in front of the station, not with all those buses and taxis. Normally, I listened to the radio while I was driving, but I didn't dare let go of the wheel. Pernille remained silent. She turned away from me. I pulled up at the bottom of the car park where there were no other cars.

'Goodbye,' I said. 'I'll let you know when I'm ready to clear out the room.'

Again, Pernille said nothing. Nothing audible, anyway. The rain bucketed down. I watched her in the rear-view mirror as she ran towards the station building. Adorable, I thought to myself. Had I ever been like that? Beyond perfect. Pluperfect. Now she was crossing the road. Maybe she'd be hit by a car! But no car hit her.

11

Ubi pus, ibi evacua.
(Where there is pus, evacuate it.)

Medical aphorism

'I took the liberty of putting some coffee on!' said Funder. He stood in the kitchen as if he belonged there.

'Let me do it properly,' I said, turning off the kettle. The lighter didn't work when I tried to turn on the gas.

'Perhaps you need a new flint,' Funder said.

'Have you got a match?' He hadn't, but then the lighter sparked. 'We're out of gas, dammit!'

'You're not allowed to use bottled gas in the kitchen any more.' The detective opened the cupboard. 'Have you got a refill?'

I nodded and gestured in the direction of the garden shed. I had changed the canister myself before and felt I needed to show him my competence. I went out through the utility room and opened the back door. The rain came down in sheets. On my way to the shed, I realized that I had forgotten the empty canister. But I was too embarrassed to turn back. The refill was heavy. I struggled to tip it over and roll it along on its rim. By the time I returned Funder had detached the empty canister. I shook the rain off me like a dog, just for fun and because I felt awkward. I wanted him to connect the refill for me, but I didn't have the courage to ask him. Suddenly my wet shoes slipped on the floor. I grabbed Funder's elbow and he reached for my shoulders but was unable to get a proper hold. I just stopped myself from falling. *Oh, kiss me, kiss me, kiss me.* I began to cry. 'And I've broken a tooth!' I wailed. Funder helped me to a chair. I didn't look at him. I wasn't really crying; I merely shed some tears. The detective busied himself with the gas.

'Making any headway with the investigation?' I finally asked.

Not much news. They knew where the killer had stood – at the far end of the churchyard on the other side of the bank, under cover of some trees. No one had actually seen him. Halland's phone had gone missing. And what about his computer?

'He had a laptop,' I said, 'but it's not here. I haven't seen his grey shoulder bag either.'

'And the keys we found in his pocket?'

'No idea,' I said.

'Halland was a lot older than you, no?'

He was. Halland would have been sixty in a few months. We had talked, rather painfully, about celebrating. We rarely invited guests after his illness. And now I didn't feel like talking to anyone about his death. Thirty-seven emails – and not one that deserved a reply.

'Was he married before?'

Halland was never married. He had a number of relation-ships, but I didn't want to know about them.

'Did he never mention particular women?'

'No. Well, yes. But no one I knew. Do you think some old flame could have shot him?'

Finishing his coffee, Funder stood up. 'Do you mind if I look around in the loft? I won't disturb anything.'

'I thought you'd already looked there.'

'I did. But I'd like to look again.' On his way up the stairs, he called back down to me, 'I've reconnected your landline. Both your plugs had been pulled out of the sockets.'

I sat in the kitchen and tried to follow the detective in my mind. What would he find? What *could* he find? There was very little in the desk, I knew. Was that normal? Did I even know? Of course I did, I just couldn't remember. Did I remember anything? I hadn't even realized that the computer was missing. I only admired Halland's sense of order. Was the desk usually that empty, or had he recently cleared out the papers?

I had twisted my back when I slipped in the kitchen. Hobbling out onto the doorstep after Funder had gone, I inhaled the clear air. The rain had stopped. The man from the jetty crossed the square. As he approached my neighbour's door, he smiled wryly and put the key into the lock. He was starting to annoy me.

'Are you staying with Brandt?' I asked. The question was stupid. He clearly had a key.

The man said nothing.

12

Dreaming softens you and makes you unfit for daily work.
Henriette Heise (quoting Louise Bourgeois), *Installation*

I stood on the tree-lined promenade that runs along the fjord.
The limes were coming into leaf. Evening light played on the
gently rippling water. A tongue probed inside my sleeve, lick-
ing my wrist. Startled, I cried out.

'He's just being friendly.' A man's voice. Brandt, the doctor,
my neighbour.

'Now that's news! I didn't know you owned a dog.' I only
spoke after he had pulled his pet to heel.

'I'm looking after him for my sister,' Brandt said from beneath
the trees.

'So you've had guests too.' I turned back to the fjord, disgusted
by the wetness on my wrist. I didn't want him to see me wipe
it off.

'Bess, I'm so sorry about Halland. Dreadful!'

'Yes.'

'I saw him.'

'You were there? On the square?'

'I saw you as well.'

My feet felt cold. 'I didn't see anyone.'

'Have the police found anything?'

'No.'

'An old friend's staying with me. He's researching photographs in the museum archives. Perhaps you've seen him?'

'We've said hello. He takes a lot of strolls for someone who's meant to be busy.'

'I've been thinking of having you round … How are you?'

The fjord had become a blend of blues and greens.

'When's the funeral?'

'Funeral?' The concept seemed beyond me.

'Won't there be one?'

I felt like saying, 'How should I know?' Stupid but true. I supposed there would be a funeral. But what was I meant to do? How did one go about getting people buried?

'The detective's been round, then?' Brandt said.

'Yes, he's been round. If that's what you want to call it. Do you know him?'

'We've met.'

'Who's your friend, when he's not spying on people?'

'Sorry about that. He told me he'd seen Funder, that's all. Surely you must agree that the whole thing's most alarming.' His eyes shone very blue.

'You should get yourself a straw hat,' I said, 'being so chic and all.' He shook his head. 'Don't you remember when we had that argument?' I asked.

'We've never had an argument!' he protested.

'You shouted at me and said I should write books *about* something!'

'We were drunk!'

'I wasn't.'

'I *was*.'

'We disagreed about which battles are worth fighting.'

'We did?'

'You and Halland.'

'*We walk in the gloaming as we sleep,*' Brandt quoted.

He now stood close to me. He was real. He smelled sweet and sour.

'I don't sleep any longer,' I said.

'I think you can.'

The dog whimpered. Brandt unhooked its lead so it could run down to the water's edge. The fjord glowed a dull green.

13

This is a stone for Hartvig Mathisen,
Born in eighteen ninety-eight.
Died the fifth of November, nineteen hundred and twelve.
And the words say he's gone, but not forgotten.
Fourteen, he was, this little Hartvig
Until he was gone, but not forgotten.
Like as not, he'd plans for life.
None can know the dreams he'd begotten ...

Song by Niels Hausgaard

Ten days had passed. I had spoken to Funder about Halland's body as though discussing a stack of books, and to the pastor as though Halland were still alive. I had also spoken to an undertaker. I couldn't avoid the undertaker. Halland was to be buried on the Friday at two o'clock. Inger and Brandt would act as pall-bearers; the pastor would find a couple of others. I avoided involving Pernille. I just left a message on her cell phone giving the time and place. I had done my duty, if that's what it was. I was exhausted, so I went to bed early. Unable to sleep, I got up and went through Halland's drawers again but found nothing new. Had his desk always been this empty? And where was his laptop? I went back downstairs and read through my own files. What a lot to throw away. Sorting and binning, I became immersed in matters of no consequence: scribbled notes, receipts, letters, newspaper cuttings – my life.

When I looked up, a red stripe hung across the morning sky. Rising to my feet, I realized that I was holding Halland's coffee mug. I had never used it before.

'*The night had passed!*' I said the words out loud, then cleared my throat and repeated them to myself. That was the hymn I had proposed to the pastor.

Pluperfect. Gazing out of the window, I rolled the words softly round my tongue.

I had studied elementary Latin at school. How much had stuck? *Italia terra est, sumus estis sunt* – the grammar trickled back – *sum es est. Pluperfect, gerund.* Such lovely words. Why did I ever enter that world of Latin words? What benefit had I derived? The answer was obvious. The world of Latin words had benefited me greatly back then, and sometimes still did. And yet, the futility of everything had become my new hobby horse. Why the fuss when all would soon be over anyway? Did anything really matter? Work, eating, sleeping? Love? Procreation?

Through the window I could just see the corner of the jetty where I had recently sat. As I pictured myself out there, a chill ran through me. An easy target for someone with a rifle in the gardens above the fjord. Who had shot Halland? Would that person also shoot me? Why wasn't I totally preoccupied with this thought? Why wasn't I frightened? The moment passed. No one would shoot me. No one would shoot Halland, come to that. But someone had.

Halland's coffee mug was blue. I put it into the kitchen sink and took his antique aquavit glass down from the shelf. I remembered buying it in Sweden. This lovely small piece had cost me twenty-five kroner. The sides slanted gently, and there was an air bubble in the base. Halland always liked an aquavit in the morning, though he never drank otherwise. I filled the glass to the brim with water and downed the lot in one. Then I went to bed and slept for most of the day. I felt safer waiting until evening to leave the house.

'Where's the dog?' I recognized Brandt's figure in the dim light on the path.

'Rushing about down by the fjord. He'll be back in a minute,' he said, turning to walk with me. We strolled along, keeping our distance.

'You know,' I said, 'I've been wondering where Halland's letters are.'

'What do you mean?'

'The thought just occurred to me so I wanted to express it.'

'Are Halland's letters missing?'

'I don't know. I always thought he had lots of documents and letters, but his desk is empty. It's as though he cleared the place out.'

'Perhaps he knew he was going to die?'

'No. I was just thinking out loud, that's all. How can anyone know they're going to be shot?'

Silence.

'Do you know something about Halland that I don't?'

'How am I supposed to answer that?'

'Do you?'

'I don't think so.'

The fjord lay still. A half-moon shone through the treetops, and dark clouds drifted across the sky. I could hear Brandt's gentle breathing, sensed his presence without looking at him.

'I love the fjord,' I said, and held my breath.

'Yes,' he said, putting his hand on my neck. We had almost reached the churchyard gates. It was dark. His hand felt so good.

'Did you shoot him?' I whispered. Brandt kept his hand in place. I thought I heard him whisper my name. When he bent his head towards mine, his breath felt warm against my face. I couldn't see him properly. My mouth touched his, he gave a start. Then the dog barked.

'You should have him on the lead in a churchyard,' I said.

'Is that where we're headed?' Brandt sounded as if he had lost his voice.

The dog sniffed at me, sticking its nose deep into my groin. I felt a cold sweat. It will bite me. It will not. Brandt attached the lead.

The churchyard gate creaked appropriately. The moon emerged from behind clouds.

'Will Halland be buried here?'

'In the new part, I imagine. Whoever shot him must have been standing here on the bank. Funder said they had found the spot. I wish the shooting had been an accident, but they think that's unlikely.'

The dog whined, then pulled sharply on the lead, causing Brandt to lurch forward.

'Because he was shot in the heart?'

'Shooting parties tend not to frequent churchyards.'

'On the other hand ...' said Brandt, and stopped walking. I could hardly see him; the moon had disappeared again.

'What?'

'There was some trouble last year, don't you remember? I'll call the chairman of the Churchyard Committee first thing.'

'Church Committee?'

'Churchyard Committee. The chairman,' he said.

'Who the hell is he when he's not chairing the Churchyard Committee?'

Brandt recoiled in surprise. 'Don't swear!' he whispered.

I couldn't help but laugh. 'Because we're in a churchyard?'

'Just don't.'

The moon reappeared.

'The funeral's on Friday,' I said. 'He wanted to be buried. I don't want anything extra, nothing at all. No death notice, no nibbles afterwards.'

'What about the booksellers, his publisher? Do they know he's dead?'

'I'm sure they read the papers. Anyway, his cell phone's gone, so I haven't got their numbers. I hadn't given them a moment's thought, to tell you the truth. I can't be bothered. I know so little about what he did, and …'

Brandt put his arm through mine. It felt right.

'I won't do it!'

'Do what?' he asked.

'Whatever they expect me to do. I won't!'

14

'Do tell me, why have you never married, Mr. Burton?' (. . .)
'Shall we say,' I said, rallying, 'that I have never met the
right woman?'
'We can say so,' said Mrs. Dane Calthrop, 'but it wouldn't
be a very good answer, because so many men have obviously
married the wrong woman.'

Agatha Christie, *The Moving Finger*

Troels had gone grey and let his hair grow long. He had become
pudgy. No substance. We hadn't seen each other for ages. I was
taken aback. He said that Abby was fine; after that I didn't listen.
I showed him into the house, which he had never seen before,
and made some tea. We sat down across from one another.

'What a dreadful thing,' he said. 'I've been thinking about
you a lot.'

'Yes, all right!' I blurted out like a child.

'You haven't changed.'

Which was a lie. Although perhaps he wasn't referring to my
appearance but to the 'Yes, all right!' We stared into space for a
while. The silence didn't bother me in the slightest. He took a
deep breath.

'Will you go to bed with me?' he asked.

'What?' I spluttered, trying to make light of his remark. I was
perfectly aware of what he had said. 'No! What *are* you thinking?'

He didn't seem embarrassed. 'I always thought I'd ask you
when Halland wasn't around any more.'

'Wasn't around any more?'

'Yes. I hadn't counted on him getting shot, though!'

'Really?'

I noticed a muscle twitching in his cheek while the rest of his face remained impassive. When we were young, the twitching muscle had fascinated me. I fantasized about it, analyzed his personality in light of it, convinced that the profundity of his personality lay there.

You were so dull and I was so bored, I thought to myself, feeling a sudden relief wash over me, as though I had spoken the words out loud. 'I understand why you ask. But I'm amazed.'

'Don't worry,' he said. 'It doesn't matter.' He wedged his tongue behind his teeth. So it *did* matter.

'I could make something of this, you making a proposition when I've just been – does the word *widowed* apply when a person wasn't married? But I haven't really got to grips with Halland's death. People in my situation talk all sorts of rubbish and do the strangest things. Yesterday, for instance, I kissed my neighbour.'

'Really?' Troels livened up.

'Yes. I haven't a clue why, but last night kissing seemed the obvious thing to do. How are your twins?'

He looked confused. His hair wasn't actually long; he just hadn't had it cut in a while. He looked dishevelled.

'I miss you,' he said.

'I don't believe you.'

'I know. The twins are noisy.'

'Yes.' I pictured them in my mind, although I had never seen them.

15

(As though unnerved by death
The black horse pulls the sleigh,)
And icicles long and piked
Suspended above the way

Emil Aarestrup, *Sleigh Ride*

I told the pastor I would arrive an hour before the funeral, but I didn't manage. My clothes weren't right, a plate needed washing. I opened and closed windows. Then there was a tiny pink rose, one of the wild ones Halland had planted. I had to cut the flower for him. 'Only neighbours will come,' I said to the pastor. 'I'm not announcing anything in the paper.' He disagreed. 'Halland's death has already been reported in the papers. The news has even been on the television!' But he didn't force the issue. And he understood when I said I didn't want any speeches about Halland's personality or achievements.

When I finally left the house, a drizzle was falling, so I grabbed an umbrella. I knew that all the neighbours would be watching. I kept my head down. I had to pass the spot where Halland had fallen to the ground. I didn't stop but slowed my steps. I had no wish to dwell on his death in front of an audience, assuming there was one.

A surprising number of cars were parked outside the church. Someone stood in the doorway and ushered people in. Pernille. Behind her a long row of wreaths and flowers stretched down the aisle. Half the pews were full.

'Bess!' she said, and opened her arms as if to embrace me. 'Where on earth have you been?' I shook my umbrella and showered her with raindrops. She was forced to step back so I could squeeze past her enormous belly. Sudden rage surged up inside me. 'Who do you think you are!' I hissed. Then I saw the coffin. And with that came the thought of Halland inside it. I stepped into the church holding the tiny pink rose. Looking straight ahead, I strode down the aisle to the coffin, placed the flower on the lid and then edged my way along the front pew without looking at anyone. Who were all these people? After a while I realized that the pastor was trying to attract my attention.

'Where do all these people come from?' I whispered angrily.

'Halland's daughter placed a notice in the paper yesterday. Didn't you see it?'

I wasn't keeping up with the newspapers. His daughter! Who did she think she was?

'She's not Halland's *daughter!*' I said loudly.

'In that case, apologies are called for. I must have got the wrong end of the stick …' The pastor glanced towards the entrance with a bewildered look on his face. His glasses slid down his nose and he pushed them back into place.

The bells rang, the door was closed and the organ struck up. Pernille sat down beside me. I slid away from her. She slid with me. Was she stupid or what?

'I suppose you arranged for nibbles at the Postgården too?' I hissed.

'Nibbles?' This was going to be an ordeal. 'Did you notice we had our picture taken?'

'When?'

'There were some photographers outside.'

I hadn't noticed. Forcing myself to concentrate on the coffin, I found my place in the hymn book and ignored her as best I could. I would be furious with her later. Not now. Later.

16

Arthur's father and I lived no further apart, with half the globe between us, than we were together in this house.
Charles Dickens, *Little Dorrit*

A person can be matte and shiny at the same time. Halland was just that. His eyes were closed when I ran into the hospital and found him on a gurney in a corridor without even a screen around him. I didn't know if he was asleep. I saw his matte and shiny face and his closed eyes and thought he was a stranger. We had been living together for more than a year, yet I had never told him that I thought about Abby every day and that I kept wondering if I had made the right decision in the first place. Every single day. I told him about my writing – a little bit – and about books and shopping, and about people I met in town. We were getting to know the neighbours, and I told him about them. Now he was lying on a gurney in a hospital corridor and didn't even know I was there. He suffered too much pain. He couldn't hear me yelling at the nurses to find somewhere else to put him, to get him a doctor, to *do something*. And he was oblivious when I threatened to contact a journalist I knew on one of the tabloids. I didn't know any tabloid journalists. A lie. But it helped.

The porter wheeled him along without looking at me. I held Halland's cold, damp hand. I couldn't talk to him with the porter there, so I squeezed his hand.

They said he had woken up. But when I went in to see him he just lay there. I sat down and waited. His breathing was laboured.

The sun shone through the window; I felt hot and nearly fell asleep. Then, without turning his head, without even opening his eyes, he said, 'The anaesthetist asked where I wanted to go. He told me to imagine somewhere I was happy. I said, "On a bus." They all laughed, but he said, "A bus it is, then!"'

At first I said nothing. I didn't think he was properly awake. We had hardly ever been on buses together.

'Was it a nice journey?' I asked eventually.

Nodding, he turned his head to look at me. 'I was there straight away, on the back seat. With you. You put your head in my lap.'

Oh, how I loved Halland at that moment. At that moment the memory returned.

17

I see you lead a double life.
There'll be an extra charge for that.

A fortune-teller

When I stood up to follow the coffin out of the church, I bowed my head to avoid looking at anyone. Brandt didn't seem to have come. Was he angry with me? Was he embarrassed? Though there were plenty of pall-bearers, some confusion arose around the coffin. The pastor stepped in and sorted it out. I stared at the various feet as I waited to leave the pew. I didn't want to be a bearer. I imagined breaking down, yet I kept myself together. I felt only a little pain in the hip but stayed in one piece. Pernille was beside me and I didn't try to get away. There were clicking sounds as if someone was taking pictures, but I wouldn't look up. We sang 'There is a lovely land.' I had nothing to toss into the grave. Thus I took Pernille's arm and steered her out through the gate onto the square. A voice, Inger's perhaps, called out to us, but I kept going.

'Do you have your bag?' I asked Pernille.

'Yes,' she replied, yelping as she stumbled in her high heels.

'Good. I'm driving you home!'

'Now?'

'Yes.'

'All the way?'

'Yes.'

In the car, I pretended that she wasn't with me. Otherwise I couldn't have driven to Copenhagen. I turned on the radio and found what I normally would have regarded as the most insufferable station imaginable. I sang along as best I could, even when I had no idea what they were playing. Pernille shrank back in her seat. Eventually she said, 'You need to fill up with gas.' She was right.

'Have you got a licence?'

'Yes.'

'Then let's swap over at the services.'

She could talk and drive at the same time, and she had that way of checking the mirror that I so admired. 'I thought there was supposed to be coffee and a bite to eat after a funeral,' she said, checking the mirror again. 'Not after this one,' I replied.

'I went to a funeral once, and afterwards over coffee people stood up and said nice things about the deceased. I found that so touching.'

'What would you have said about Halland?'

'I wouldn't,' she said. 'But I've been thinking about something since he died. After I fell pregnant, I became rather unhinged. I told him I didn't want to see him any more, that I wanted him to move his stuff out. That made him cry.'

Halland didn't know how to cry. I never saw a tear in his eye, not once, not even a snivel. A slight flutter in his voice on occasion, then a deep breath and he regained control.

'I feel so bad about asking him to leave, because I didn't really want that. But everything was such a mess, and I need my baby to have the right start.'

'But you can't afford the rent without Halland's help,' I said. 'Wasn't that what you told me the other day?'

'Yes, and in fact I didn't want to throw him out. I just wasn't thinking straight at the time. We worked things out in the end.'

Halland didn't know how to cry. I didn't believe her.

'Did Halland need to leave for the baby to have the right start?'

'I told you, I wasn't thinking straight!'

'So you keep saying.'

The apartment was big for someone on their own; I could see why Pernille had rented out a room. While I waited in the hallway, she disappeared into the bathroom. 'Do you have the keys?' she called out.

'Yes, they've been in my pocket for days, bloody things,' I muttered, pulling them out. 'Which room is it?'

'First on the left, the one with the door closed!' Emerging from the bathroom, she came and stood behind me as if to follow me into the room. Turning round I said, 'I'll tell you if I need you!'

'Please yourself! Do you want something to drink?'

'Have you got any aquavit or whisky? Anything strong. Just a single glass.'

'I'll have a look.'

I unlocked Halland's room, stepped inside and closed the door behind me. My gaze fell on a film poster that hung on the wall between the windows: *Le Retour de Martin Guerre*. I sat down on the bed and stared. 'That's not funny!' I said to Gérard Depardieu.

At home Halland had hung up a couple of reproductions. This poster was so enormous that the room nearly capsized. The bed was narrow and prim. A white cover was tucked in neatly at the corners. On top lay a large pillow. His laptop stood on the desk with the lid open, the screen blank. Books were stacked in a deep-shelved bookcase rather than lined up in rows. There were piles of documents. On the floor stood three packing cases with their flaps open. Papers had been thrown into each of them without much thought. There was a clothes rail with hangers, a jacket and two white shirts.

'Halland?'

'I have some aquavit as it happens!' said Pernille, entering the room with a bottle and a glass in her hands.

'Out!' I shouted. 'I don't want any aquavit! Make me some coffee! If you've got decent coffee, that is!'

'I beg your pardon,' she huffed, and went away again. The door didn't shut properly behind her. Did it stand ajar like that when Halland was here, so his life could seep out into hers, and hers into his? Sighing, I stared wearily at the packing cases. What was I doing here? What had I been thinking? Would I have to lug all this down to the car? I wanted none of it. But I supposed I'd better have a look, if only I could get up. Then I could bin the lot.

'Pernille!' I called. She appeared in the doorway at once. 'Do you know anything about all this?'

She glanced around. 'It's not normally untidy. Those boxes are new. I guess the rest is work.'

'If I pay the rent, can the papers stay here for a while?'

'The longer you pay the rent, the less I have to worry about! Do you want a hand?'

'With what?' I stared at the piles.

'Don't the papers all need sorting?'

'But we don't know what any of it is!'

Was I meant to ask if Halland was the father of Pernille's child? I wouldn't. How could Halland have fathered a child? That made no sense. Then why did I assume the baby was his? I had no reason. With whom was I angry? And what did

Halland think he was doing putting up that poster, a poster for a film dealing with the most celebrated, most lamentable, most improbable case of imposture the world had ever seen. A film that was all the more improbable for ending happily. Halland had told me about that film so often. He loved it. I watched it once for his sake, but he watched it a thousand times. What was he thinking? Had he ever imagined that one day I would be sitting on this bed, unable to get up, glaring at a French actor?

Pernille knelt with difficulty beside one of the packing cases, gingerly lifted out a few documents and envelopes and began to read. I closed my eyes and listened. Sounds filtered up from the street. Cars drove through rain, buses pulled in and out. These were the sounds that had accompanied Halland to sleep. I always thought he stayed in a hotel when he visited Copenhagen. I knew about his life in provincial hotels; he had told me all about it. But what was *this*?

'How long did you say Halland kept this room?' My eyes were closed.

'I didn't.'

'I might not be able to afford the rent ...'

'Perhaps you won't ...' Pernille said dreamily, as people do when they are reading and not listening. I glanced down at her. 'What have you've found?' I asked. She looked up in annoyance. 'I'm not sure. A travel journal, I think.'

'Halland didn't keep a journal.'

'No,' she said. I closed my eyes again.

'What does it say?' I asked.

'Nothing. There's all sorts of things here, notebooks, letters, manuscripts.'

'All that stuff was in his desk.'

'What?'

'Nothing.'

'Yuck.' She tossed a black notebook onto the bed. I flipped it open with one finger. 'That's not Halland's handwriting.'

'I can see that.'

'Why did you say "yuck"?'

'Read it yourself,' she replied.

'Do you mind if I have a nap? You don't have to do all that.' Lying down on my side, I pushed the pillow onto the floor and pulled the cover over me. I fell asleep at once.

When I opened my eyes, Pernille's face was hovering above mine. 'What's the matter?' she asked.

'What?' I spluttered. I had no idea where I was.

'You were dreaming! I'll make you that coffee.' She left the room. The bedcover was wet beside my mouth. Turning over, I looked across at Halland's desk. There were neat piles on it now. I sat up. The computer would have to come back with me; the detective would want it. I felt no urge to pry. My natural curiosity had vanished the moment I found the keys to the room.

I looked through the black notebook that Pernille had flung on my bed.

It's the most wonderful thing. The dream of happiness come true. This is amazing, indescribable, it's ...

'Yuck,' I said, and put it aside.

Pernille returned with a cup of black coffee. The smell woke me up.

'Isn't it gross?' she asked, and edged past me. She sat down on the bed.

'What do you do exactly? I said. 'I didn't know that you were interested in literature.'

'Oh, but I'm not,' she said, and then she started laughing. 'Actually I am. I work in a bookshop just along there.' She jerked her thumb over her shoulder. Her laugh showed her off well and I laughed alongside. Laughter has never suited me; I always cover my mouth if I remember to. 'But that's not literature,' she said. I agreed.

'I was having a nightmare, and now I've forgotten the subject. I have a sort of *Bluebeard* feeling that I've dropped the key and stained it with indelible blood. I hate prying into other people's stuff. Thank you for doing all of this.'

She shrugged and sipped her coffee. 'What's *Bluebeard*?' she asked.

'You don't know what nibbles are either,' I said. 'Not doing very well, are we?'

Her nostrils flared. 'You're not prying. It's just words on paper. Halland has been murdered. There might be something important here.'

For a moment we sat silently together on Halland's bed. 'I'll take the computer back with me. And Martin Guerre.'

'What?'

'Him!' I pointed up at the wall.

'You'll have a job taking that down!'

'Down it's coming, all the same.'

'There's something else you should take with you. I had it in my bag when I came to see you, but you sent me packing.'

Just for a moment, I had forgotten what happened before and thought how kind she was. Now I began to grumble again. The death notice in the newspaper. Who did she think she was?

'What is it?' I asked.

'His mail.'

His mail.

'I don't know why, but he had his mail forwarded here.'

'Since when?' Now I was angry again.

Struggling to her feet, she left the room, then returned with a stack of envelopes. Mostly bills, by the look of them. Placing them in my lap, I stared at the redirection notice. A permanent change of address, commencing two weeks before he died.

I looked at Pernille standing there, her legs apart, trying to catch her breath.

'Why would he do that?' I demanded.

'No idea. I was going to ask him the next time he came.'

'Did he want to move in with you?'

Her eyes glazed over. 'What do you want me to say? You wouldn't believe me anyway.'

'Try me.'

'He never actually said that he wanted to and I don't believe he would have done. But I can't be sure.'

I got up and went over to the desk. There was an old photo on top of one of the piles. As I reached for it, Pernille said, 'Isn't that a lovely picture? It's Halland as a boy – with a maverick!'

Without so much as a glance in her direction, I crumpled the photograph in my hand. *Maverick indeed.*

'What are you doing?!' she burst out.

'None of your business!' I said. 'I'm leaving. I need to get these things down to the car, and then I'll be off.'

'And you will drive yourself?'

I didn't reply.

18

*'And all the while, I suppose,' he thought, 'real people were
living somewhere, and real things happening to them ...'*
Edith Wharton, *The Age of Innocence*

Halfway home I stopped at a service station for a sandwich
consisting of meat and a disgusting white undefinable spread.
Sitting in the fading light and watching people fill up with gas
in the dreary weather, I drank a bottle of water. Then I switched
on the car's interior light. Martin Guerre was rolled up length-
wise on the back seat. On the passenger seat lay Halland's
computer bag, his redirected mail and the black notebook. 'The
most wonderful thing, indeed!' I flicked through the pages again,
skimming over entries describing a journey. A firm hand, blue
ballpoint pen, no dates, just days of the week.

> *We're sitting waiting at a dark station, looking forward to
> going home, though no one awaits us there, or because no one
> awaits us there; we're self-contained, as everyone should be
> allowed to be once or twice in their lives. We had bought some
> things for a picnic: a bottle of wine, a crusty loaf, two types
> of cheese, fragrant tomatoes that burst and drip. We had a
> compartment to ourselves, and when the conductor asked to
> see our tickets we were already half drunk and in high spirits;
> I imagined him rather envious in a friendly sort of way. He
> explained something I understood, but I didn't let it sink in. I
> thought we had plenty of time, and anyway we had to eat the*

food first. When I staggered out to the toilet, the wine and the train and the joy made me uncertain on my feet. And to my great delight I deposited the biggest, most well-formed turd I had ever seen into the toilet bowl. I looked at it with content-ment and was only sorry that I couldn't tell anybody about it. And then, just as I was about to let it slide from the bowl onto the tracks below, I realized that we were standing at a station. Flushing the toilet was forbidden. On my way back to the compartment I passed only empty seats; I opened a window in the corridor and stuck my head out to see how far we'd come, then called out that – according to the conductor's orders – we must go to the front of the train. We ran as fast as we could with the suitcase and clutching the food, but we were too late. At the end of the carriage we came to nothing. We had been uncoupled and the rest of the train had left. And yet we were happy; it was the most wonderful thing.

I recognized the handwriting. I couldn't breathe. That's enough. Secret pregnant nieces. Secret rooms. And what kind of secret was this? Maverick? I know what goes on in Halland's mind. I fell in love with him, of course I know. I can read his slightest passing thought; I can sense him without touching. I can hear the modulations in his voice when we speak on the phone, and I know exactly what each of them means. Such is true love.

It was time to go home. I got out of the car and strode across to a bin and dropped in the bottle and sandwich wrapper. I liked the smell of service stations. A smell that could make me cry.

The rest of the way home, I sang snippets of all the hymns I could remember, and when the words ran out I sang on unabated: Halland, oh Halland, oh why and wherefore, and glorious Halland, oh Halland, ha ha, and ye noble Martin

Guerre, oh Halland the dwarf, a riddle was he, what is it that leaves and never comes back ...

I parked on the square and sat for a while before opening the car door. My hands were sore from gripping the wheel. I had avoided the funeral reception that never was. I thought no one would be at the church besides Inger and Brandt, and they could have come back for coffee in my kitchen. The flowers and wreaths must have been placed on the grave. Wasn't that customary? I wanted to see if they were there, though it was nearly dark.

But I never got that far. I could just make out the flowers – the white ones were still visible, even in the gathering darkness – but I had a strange feeling. Turning my head, I listened. Footsteps? Someone running? The sound of my own breathing drowned out what I might have heard. I tried to stop breathing and found I couldn't. But there *were* footsteps. There *was* someone running. And then I ran myself, as fast as I could, to the churchyard exit. The heavy gate creaked.

19

Come on in — there's nobody in here but me and a big blue-bottle fly.

Raymond Chandler, *The Little Sister*

I opened the door. Brandt's lodger. I haven't described him. I won't bother now; it's irrelevant.

'Have you seen Brandt?' he asked. Lowering my gaze, I stepped aside so that he could come in. I had slept for hours but cried so much in my dreams that I felt exhausted.

The lodger had expected Brandt the day before. Having made dinner, he thought the doctor must have been delayed at the surgery. But Brandt never came. So the lodger ate his dinner, did the washing-up and waited. Then he called the surgery and Brandt's cell phone several times, but either he reached an answering machine or made no connection. He slept badly and was unsure whether to report the doctor as missing to the police.

Brandt's hand on my neck. Dusk. I was looking forward to seeing him again. My stomach hurt. 'Do sit down,' I said. 'Life ends so abruptly,' I ventured. 'Or can do.'

'Do you think he might be dead?' The lodger hadn't shaved. The shadow of his stubble made his features all the more prominent.

'Of course not!' I said. 'Can I offer you a wee dram?' I heard the voice of my grandfather in my own. He always offered his guests a wee dram.

Brandt was a grown-up. We didn't need to worry about him. So we drank one aquavit and then another. We chatted about Brandt, about how unlike him it was not to call. But today was a Saturday and his day off. Polite conversation between strangers. The aquavit helped, but not much. The drink was sharp yet smooth on the tongue, with a taste of caraway and aniseed, but mostly of alcohol. I sipped, then knocked the rest back in one.

'Would you like another?' I asked.

'Perhaps he met a woman on his way home from work,' the lodger suggested, sounding unconvinced.

'Perhaps he did,' I said, looking out onto the square. 'Perhaps he met a woman.'

There was a dead fly on the windowsill, a lot of dust and some mysterious black spots.

'He didn't come to the church yesterday either,' I said. 'I found that odd, but thought I knew why.'

'Was the funeral yesterday? He didn't mention it.'

I went to the phone and called Brandt's secretary, but no one answered. The lodger looked out of sorts. Perhaps he needed a cigarette.

'And then there's the dog,' he said.

'Is it still at Brandt's house?'

'Yes. I don't care for dogs much, but I took his for a walk.'

'He can't have met a woman, then,' I said. 'Not while he's looking after a dog.'

'Which he isn't any longer,' the lodger replied.

20

With the carefree ingratitude that becomes spoiled children
so well, the boy reaches out for the marmalade, while Mrs.
Andersen, who always smells so chastely of soap and ironing,
carefully removes the shell from his egg.

Tove Ditlevsen, *Vilhelm's Room*

When the lodger had gone, I drank another shot of aquavit.
After that I stared out of the window, then rang Brandt's cell
phone. No answer. Wedging Inger's casserole dish under my
arm, I went next door and knocked. I could hear raised voices
inside, hers and Lasse's. I rang the doorbell, though I knew it
didn't work, then knocked again.

'I won't put up with it for one more minute!' Inger yelled in
my face, stepping past me into the square.

'He's just a teenager,' I mumbled.

'That doesn't excuse *everything*! I'm sick to *bloody death* of him.
Never lifts a finger, lounging about all day ... He was supposed to
help me this morning, but he's only just crawled out of bed with a
hangover. He thinks he's going out again tonight. How can you get
drunk when you're seventeen anyway? Isn't it against the law?'

'Just leave him,' I said, and went inside. Lasse sat in the
kitchen, slumped in front of a bowl of porridge and a glass of
chocolate milk.

'Got a headache, have we?' I chuckled. Hangovers are funny
at that age. They're proud of them. 'You haven't seen Brandt, I
suppose, either of you? His lodger says he's gone missing.'

They hadn't. And didn't seem that bothered either. I watched Lasse. He was so listless, so boyish and self-conscious. A few moments ago he had yelled at his mother. She was still livid.

'He takes and takes and never gives anything in return!' she fumed. Lasse cowered. I wanted a teenager at home, even an unreasonable one. As unreasonable as they came – I wouldn't mind. Not everyone is cut out for children, but most people have them anyway. As always, I was overcome by a rather gratu-itous tenderness since I had no children living with me. Besides, Abby would be twenty-four soon. But there had been a time when she was small, just growing up. A time when she laughed and cried, played on the swing, spilt her food down her front; a time when she immersed herself in play, sat still to have her hair brushed; a time of sleeping and waking; a time of singing and shouting and squealing with joy; a time of whispered secrets and finishing her dinner; a time of pulling faces, and dealing out kisses, and shying away from kisses offered in return. I wanted it all back, yet at the time the opportunity seemed to have passed me by. When I wept from the pain of not having Abby, I really wept for not being a decent mother. I had been a hypocrite who had wanted Abby to like me. But she couldn't. It was as simple as that. I often thought of how I held her in my arms as a baby just as I recently held my cousin's sleeping newborn grandchild. I sat and gazed into that little face, longing to relive the entire experience, even the part where Abby started answering back as children do. I even wanted her to despise me again because she would at least be with me. I had made one of my despairing attempts at becoming a decent mother after reading an article claiming that mealtimes delivered many benefits. One had to make an effort with the table, for example by using colourful napkins. The first time I tried this, I don't think Abby or her father noticed. In fact, Abby tried to pick a fight and her first mouthful prompted the obnoxious comment: 'Your food tastes like shit!' Although her words upset me, I nearly burst out laughing. She noticed straight away and flew into a rage. And now I could only remember her comment and her eyes filling with tears, not the reason for her anger. Perhaps her father and I had already decided to split up. Yes, that must have been the reason.

'What happened to you yesterday?' asked Inger. 'And who was the pregnant young thing doing the honours at the door?'

I shrugged. 'Thanks for your help at the church. I needed to get away.'

'But who was she?'

I gave Inger a look that said *later*, though I had no intention of pursuing the matter. Turning back to Lasse, I asked, 'Where are you off to tonight, then?' His mouth full, he pointed at the local paper lying open on the table in front of him. *Pavilion reopens*, it said.

'Oh,' I said. 'Can you believe it?'

Standing behind me with her hands on my shoulders, Inger read the article.

'Halland always said someone should reopen that place, and when they did we'd ...'

'We'd what?'

'Be the first ones to go. Inger! Let's go tonight, you and me. What do you say?'

'She's not going!' Lasse said.

He was right. Inger wasn't going. Moreover, she was mortified that I would even consider the idea. 'Bess,' she said. 'Do you really think that would be appropriate?'

Lasse looked displeased.

'I won't let on that I know you,' I promised him. Smiling awkwardly, he got up from the table.

'Plate!' Inger barked. Lasse moved his plate to the counter, then turned to leave the room.

'Dishwasher!' she barked again. 'And what about the glass?' But he was gone. Her face contorted and she turned away. I felt like asking her if she loved him, asking why she would yell at a child because of a plate. But I hesitated, and then she was herself again, sitting down at the table and reaching for a book that lay open. 'It's one of those books for the washroom,' she said, 'Victorian instructions for mourning. A widow was supposed to mourn her spouse for two or three years, a widower only three months. If you lost a child or a parent, you were supposed to mourn for a year. These rules may seem silly, but they make some kind of sense.'

There was a loud knock on the door. Inger leapt to her feet.

'Goodness, someone is ringing!'

'No, they're not! Isn't it time you got the bell fixed?'

'It's a quote!' she shouted from the hall. 'Beckett!'

While she spoke to the person at the door, I flicked through the washroom book.

'It was the lodger,' she announced when she came back into the kitchen. 'Asking after Brandt.'

'When did you last see him? He didn't come to the church yesterday.' I wanted to talk about something else. 'Do you know him, the lodger?'

'No. I just know that he's doing some work in the museum archives. Who was that girl yesterday? The one at the door.'

'No one. What was that Beckett quote?'

'The quote came from a play that my dad directed at his school. I was a child. I can't have been very old. The play was new then. I went round repeating the words for years. I thought they were hilarious.'

'Your dad put on Beckett at a school?'

'He did! Or maybe it wasn't Beckett. An absurd play, anyway. Bess, don't they have any idea who shot Halland?'

'They haven't told me anything.'

'Have you asked?'

'Not really. Anyway, I'm off to the Pavilion.'

'Bess, we've just buried Halland. You can't go to the Pavilion.'

'Don't make me say that Halland would have wanted me to go.'

'But there are reasons behind those mourning rules. They're for your own good.'

'Mourning …' Should I tell her that I didn't mourn for Halland? For ten years I mourned for Abby – someone I had killed and who was not even dead.

'If you don't want to come, I will go on my own,' I said.

21

The witches of my neighbourhood run the hazard of their lives upon the report of every new author who seeks to give body to their dreams.

Montaigne, *Essays*

In the beginning, before we started watching television every night, we read and talked. One evening, Halland told me about a hypnotist he had seen as a boy. The man made a group of teenagers think they were hens, but Halland didn't believe they were truly hypnotized. He still thought the man was a hoaxer.

I witnessed a similar performance by the same hypnotist, though he was older then. He convinced me, and I told Halland so. 'Why?' he asked. I had told the story so often that my reasoning had become an anecdote in its own right. But now that I wanted to tell the anecdote to Halland, the words stuck in my throat.

I was afraid that the hypnotist's power would reach out and grab me even though I sat at the back. I kept shaking my head and saying no to keep his voice and eyes away from me. Volunteers from the audience were invited onto the stage. Told to do stupid things, they obeyed. When they were handed invisible drinks, they raised their invisible glasses and looked like they were drunk. 'Now you're at a sex show!' said the hypnotist's metallic voice. 'What do you see, Hans Henrik?' Hans Henrik was a tall, skinny boy in my class who never said a word. The audience held its breath.

'It's disgusting!' he shouted in a strange, deep voice. The audience laughed.

I didn't want to reveal myself. The ambiguity of the situation frightened me. In Halland's eyes I saw how much I resembled Hans Henrik. The incident didn't appear funny any more. Halland wouldn't be amused in the right way; the anecdote could reveal insights about me I hadn't even considered. So this was another story I didn't tell him.

In the night, I screamed, 'You're touching me!'

'Where? Where?' he whispered. But whatever was happening had stopped and there was nothing more to say.

22

It is told that the mother bewailed the boy's reluctance to drink aquavit, despite her adding sugar. In his adult years, however, he caused his mother little concern in that respect.

H. P. Hansen, *Gypsies and Tinkers*

I took my bike. How did I look? At least I had a bath and put my hair up as best I could. Two long earrings dangled in unison as I pedalled. The air was warm and still. I sang softly to myself: *'Blest comfort too holds the peaceful night, when skies in the sunset glow.'* The rape fields smelt sweet. I had drunk another aquavit before leaving the house. Two, in fact. I felt like continuing to sing, but then just spoke: 'Brandt! Halland! Brandt! Halland! Where are you? Where are you? What's going on? What's happening?' I liked to repeat myself. Besides, I wasn't listening to the words. I liked the rhythm. I liked the drink talking. I was worried yet happy. At least, I felt as though I were happy. But that couldn't be true. Someone had bought the Pavilion. Why had we not heard about it? Did Halland know? We had not visited the Pavilion for a while. Two years, perhaps. Last time we took a picnic and sat on the stone bench in the overgrown garden. Now he was with me again, the dear man. The cheat, the traitor. We were entering the woods. The beech trees sported their new leaves. The sun went down and I only wobbled a bit. I could hear the music long before I arrived. Getting off my bike, I walked the rest of the way in order to savour the moment. My steps slowed. I passed a couple of laughing, tipsy youngsters who didn't appear to notice me.

As I stepped into the dim light, I recognized some faces. They all looked the other way. Only one brightened on seeing me. Lasse had apparently forgotten that we weren't going to speak to each other. As he started to walk towards me, a girl pulled him back, wanting to dance. A flat-chested young woman at the bar looked me in the eye as though she were about to say something, but she said nothing. When I pointed, she pulled me a beer.

Brandt's lodger stood in the corner furthest from the dance floor and talked to a blonde with hair down past her waist. She seemed a fun person. He laughed so heartily that I felt sure I could hear him above the music. Turning away, I sensed him. The feeling reminded me of being a teenager. I pretended not to be bothered. I was a grown-up now. His dark hair, narrow hips and angular jaw contradicted any strict notions of beauty and lent him an original air, the kind of thing that had attracted me since childhood. Not everyone had that look. Halland hadn't, neither did Troels. Here I was, standing with my back to him, knowing where he was in the room, certain that I would always know. Gulping down my beer, I asked for another and a Fernet Branca to go with it. The music was OK and I wanted to dance. The lodger and the blonde had stopped talking; she was on the dance floor now, smiling at me. I began to move towards her, but was stopped by a hand on my shoulder. I didn't recognize him at first. 'I owe you an apology!' he shouted above the noise. His speech was slurred. 'For what?' I shouted back. 'For nearly having you arrested!' It was Bjørn the caretaker, the last person to see Halland alive, or nearly so.

Surely I should've dragged him outside so we could talk in peace? Instead I shouted, 'Do you want to dance?' 'Love to!' he shouted back. While I danced with the caretaker, the lodger stood sipping a beer. He had shaved and his hips were narrow. I wanted to move closer to him, to ask him if Brandt had come home, even though I knew he hadn't. I closed my eyes to hear the music. I turned and swayed. The singer's gravelly voice kept missing the top notes, but he was good. I opened my eyes to look at him and found myself facing the wrong way. I almost fell on top of some people at a table. Bjørn the caretaker was gone. The blonde was on the other side of the room. Where was Brandt's lodger? The people at the table glared at me. The woman closest to me stood up and took me by the elbow. She wanted to lead me away, but I didn't want to go. 'Come on!' she barked, bustling me along. People stepped aside. I was going to tell her that we were like Moses parting the waves, but there was too much noise.

We went out into the foyer. The woman bundled me outside. I recognized her. She worked at the supermarket checkout. 'Best I run you home, don't you think?' she said. 'But I don't want to go home!' I protested. 'I'm sure you don't, but you really ought to.' Where had I left my bike? My tongue didn't obey me. 'My husband's just died!' I blurted out, immediately feeling angry with myself. I liked the woman so much, and here I was offending her because I was drunk. 'I know; everyone does!' 'Do they?' '*And* you're all over the papers today!' 'Am I? What for?' 'You ought to go home.' I began to snivel. 'But I don't *want* to go home!'

The woman went back inside. A boisterous group of kids were smoking a little way off. O, angular jaw! I giggled. I stepped awkwardly on the soft woodland ground. Why was the night so dark? How far had I come? The Pavilion was behind me, but there was no music. I stood in the darkness, in the silence. The air was heavy. I saw a shadow in front of me; I wasn't sure. The night was blacker than black. Had I gone blind? I closed my eyes and opened them again. No difference. Straining to hear, I put my hand out to feel my way. Was this the path? Would I walk into a tree? I felt a breath of air. Was someone breathing next to me? I stiffened, then swayed, took a step, then another. I recited out loud, 'No sound of anyone fleeing. *Darkness, darkness – the knave's head upon a plate!*' Now I was singing, aware that I was singing the song I only ever sang when I was drunk. I didn't sound pretty. I felt my way forward with my feet. This must be the path. Angular jaw. Thank goodness I got away. Away from the Pavilion. Away from myself. Where did I leave my bike? Is it summer? When will the sun come up? I felt cold and put my hands to my ears. My earrings were gone. That was always the way. I needed a pee and tried to squat down without falling over. Where was I? Warmth rose up from beneath me. Then I was bathed in a sudden, violent light. I nearly lost my balance. 'Don't shoot!' My voice rang out and everything went dark again. A car door opened and a glow shone from inside. Someone was walking towards me. Struggling to get to my feet and pulling my knickers up, I fell over into the wet. 'And I have broken a tooth!' I shouted.

23

Finally she couldn't bear it any longer. She told her secret to one of her sisters. Immediately all the other sisters heard about it. No one else knew, except a few more mermaids who told no one — except their most intimate friends.

Hans Christian Andersen, *The Little Mermaid*

'He used to come here now and again because of the sea eagles. One time he fell into the reeds. I helped him inside, didn't I? Gave him a hot toddy and a warm sweater. He had been ill and was still rather frail, but my word he was handsome! He would look in every now and then. Halland was a good-looking man, but nothing went on between us. You'd know that, of course, being his wife. What am I saying! Of course you would!'

Laughter. Peals of laughter.

'But handsome, I'll give him that. Not that I ever let on, though he may have had an inkling. Then again, he might just have felt comfortable here. I'm always one to put the coffee on. I gathered he hardly drank at all, apart from the odd beer perhaps; that was a pleasure of the past like the other thing. We could always chat, though. I've never been married myself, never had a man in the house — around the house, I mean. So it was nice. Cozy, even. Do you know, I'd squint my eyes sometimes and picture him living here. I hope you don't mind me saying this. I never told him to his face, of course. Nothing to be worried about there. Still, you know what I mean. He was frail and poorly the first couple of years. Handsome, mind! You were a lucky woman. My word!'

Laughter. Loud braying laughter.

'I'm sorry, there's nothing to laugh about. I know there isn't. I always thought you were a lucky woman. You and I never knew each other, but he talked about you all the time. Not excessively, mind. Not like he was saying things he shouldn't. He was in the dumps, you see. On your behalf, you could say. Because you were young, a lot younger. That was the thing. He'd torn you away from the life you had before, and the thought upset him. He didn't think he was much of a man any more, but of course he was. You can vouch for that. You were never wanting for anything in that department, as far as I could make out. He spoke to me in confidence, of course. I'm not sure I understood him right, because he never said it in so many words. It's more what I took him to mean, understand? I've thought about him such a lot over the years. I hope you didn't mind me turning up at the funeral? I felt I knew him better than most, you see. Next to you, of course. But then what would I know? One thing, though: I won't half miss him. You should've seen me crying when I heard the news on the radio. I was in shock, understand? I had to get on my bike and see the spot, but the police had cordoned everything off. When I went back later, there was nothing to see. Not so much as a drop of blood was left of him. Gave me the willies, it did. First he was there and then he wasn't. And then, when I saw the coffin in the church. Well, it might have been him and then again it might not. The coffin could've been empty for all anyone knew. The pastor never said a word about him other than his name, so who's to say? I didn't care for that one bit. He ought to have said a few words at least. He could've said that Halland was the most handsome man in the town. Because he was, wasn't he? And he could've said something about his birds, about all the things he knew. Or the

93

books he read. There was plenty there to be getting on with. But not a word. Always been too high and mighty by half, that pastor, if you ask me. Not that I go there much, but it's true all the same, a lot of folk say so. I'd play for him sometimes too. Just occasionally. I'm not bad, even if I say so myself. He actually paid to have the piano tuned. That was the only thing he ever gave me, mind. Just in case you were wondering. I never imagined I'd see you at the Pavilion, but I can understand why you were there. I'm in mourning myself, but that didn't stop me, did it? You were lucky I found you at all. How on earth you managed to wander so far, I'll never know. You could've lain there and died in the night if my torch hadn't picked you out on the way home. I saw you dancing and didn't have the nerve to speak to you. But when I found you there, I felt I was receiving a gift from Halland. Like the time Halland fell into the fjord. A fairy tale, it was. There you were, lying in the woods in the dark. Imagine what Halland would have made of you. Am I wrong?'

Laughter. Trickles of laughter.

'I hope you won't take this the wrong way, but like that queen once said, *We have both lost a good man*. No misunderstanding intended.'

'Sorry, I'm going to be sick,' I said, and headed for the door. I spewed everything out in front of the woman's house, making sure to spray her front step. I wasn't going back inside anyway. So there I stood, bent double and gripping the iron handrail, cold sweat on my forehead. The retching felt awful and yet, as always, came as a relief. I was shaking uncontrollably, and then there was nothing left inside me. Throwing up with nothing to throw up was the worst. After a while, the spasms stopped. Wiping my face with the back of my hand, I spat in the grass and went round the side of the house, where I found my bike leaning against the wall next to a bench. Her name was Stine. My head was pounding. How had I ended up on her sofa? Had I come on my bike? I sat down on the bench in the sun. My head didn't welcome the brightness. I shivered from coldness. I could hear Stine laughing inside the house. Did she laugh out loud when she was on her own? Was she on the telephone? 'Don't ever tell anyone this,' Halland would say sometimes. I wanted to weep. Was Stine's laughter Halland's way of taunting me? Was I meant to be his gift to this demented, cackling woman? I refused to believe he had ever felt comfortable in her company. Madness. *I'm in mourning myself!*

24

'When you've seven children to mind,' said the mother, 'there'll always be one falling down somewhere.'
William Bloch, *Travels with Hans Christian Andersen*

Jumping off my bike, I crossed the square on foot. Or perhaps I should say 'getting off': there was nothing athletic about my movement. I felt empty and at the same time heavy, as if filled with metal. I even tasted metal in my mouth. I sensed a headache coming on. And again, there was the fear, but fear of what? All part and parcel of drinking aquavit. I had been there before, with the smell of ammonia in my nostrils.

Someone was sitting on the step. As far as I could make out, it was a woman, though no one I recognized. She was reading. She could have been me. I adopted the look of disapproval I normally reserved for tourists who thought they could stand and gawk at people's windows on the square or take photographs through doors left open. I abruptly stopped in my tracks. The woman looked up. She didn't smile. But I did.

'How often do you get the cleaning done?'

Her first words after I let her into the house. She was indomitable. Cleaning was one of her talents, or at least seeing what needed doing.

'As seldom as possible,' I replied. 'I see the dirt but do nothing. I've told my cleaner I won't be needing her for the time being.'

'Just because your husband's dead doesn't mean the place has to go to pot,' she said. Indomitable, and sensible too. 'Is the house yours?'

'Not yet. But it will be.'

'How does that work?' she asked, clearly interested. But the subject was too trivial to discuss further.

'It doesn't matter. But thank you for your concern about my future.'

She looked around, surveying the walls, the piano, the bookcases, the pictures. She stopped at the portrait. 'Why have you got a picture of Frederik VI on your wall?' she asked, surprised.

I was proud that she recognized the king, but kept the reason to myself. 'It's Halland's,' I said. Wrong answer. She carried on. My study door was open. 'Is that where you work? Where was my room supposed to have been?'

'Your room's upstairs. You can stay the night if you want.'

Going over to my desk, she looked out of the window. 'A trembling mirror,' she said.

'What?'

'"The Fjord." We read the story at school. Twice. Once in primary school and then again in sixth form.'

'How original.'

'You called the fjord a trembling mirror.'

'Did I really?'

'One of the teachers said it was a cliché. His words made me angry.'

His words made her angry! 'But it *is* a cliché.'

'Yes.'

'Perhaps I stole the phrase from somewhere. It sounds alien. I don't recall writing it.'

'No.' She straightened up and turned towards me. 'This place is a dump. It reminds me of when I was little. You read that story aloud at one of your readings.'

My ears rang. 'You came to one of my readings?'

She shrugged.

'Without saying hello?'

'You didn't see me.'

'There are always so many people at those events.'

'Not at that one.'

'I'm sorry. For not recognizing you.'

She shrugged.

'I always thought I could pick you out anywhere.'

'Why?'

She stood right in front of me, looking grown-up but still so very young. Yet I knew she didn't think of herself as young. Never does a person feel so wise, so mature and so adult as when she is not. But I couldn't tell her that. She was the most beautiful creature I had ever seen. Could I tell her that? She wasn't being all that nice to me, but I didn't expect her to be.

She looked under my desk and tugged at something. When she straightened up again, she was holding the telephone lead in her hand. 'Have you pulled the plug out?' she asked. I hadn't the heart to say, 'What does it look like?' As she crawled around trying to find the phone jack, I sat down on the sofa. 'I'm a bit dizzy. I didn't sleep much last night,' I said.

'Were you out all night?' She stood in the doorway, looking mildly outraged.

'As a matter of fact I was.'

'But it's almost midday. Where have you been?'

I started to laugh, and was so taken by the sound of my own laughter that I carried on. She looked like she had discovered something unpleasant. Perhaps she could smell me.

Sitting on the edge of an armchair, she said, 'Dad's divorced now, you know. She won't let him see the twins.'

I tried to look unruffled. 'When did that happen?'

'About six months ago.'

'He never said.' Don't gawk like that, Abby, it doesn't become you. 'Have you *spoken* to him?'

'Yes. He was here.'

'Here? What for?'

'What for, indeed? We didn't get round to that. And why are *you* here? Halland's dead. I suppose that's why you're all turning up like this.'

'But Dad hates you.'

'Does he? Still? It didn't show.'

She stared emptily at Frederik VI. 'And no one's allowed to mention Halland.'

'You do as well, I suppose? Hate me?'

'Not really. I did, but I'm used to not seeing you now.'

'Have you never missed me?'

'Of course I have.'

'You said my food tasted like shit.'

She wrinkled her nose. 'I did not!'

'It doesn't matter.'

'Are you saying that's why you got divorced? Did you move in with Halland to get away from me?'

'Of course not. It's just another one of those sad things, that's all. If I'm trying to say anything, perhaps it's that being a mother isn't easy.'

'So you took off?'

'Stop it! I've missed you every single second since I left. *You* were the one . . .'

'No, *you* were, Mum.' Standing up, Abby shuddered. She had called me Mum. Now I felt emotional.

'Yes, you're right,' I said. 'It was me. Would you like something to eat?'

She smiled. She *smiled*!

'Dad really does hate you! Was he horrid when he was here?'

'Not at all. He was just . . .'

'Just what?'

'Dull?'

She laughed out loud. Oh, my daughter in my living room, laughing out loud. Why was Troels not allowed to see the twins? What was that about?

'I'm no better at cooking, but I need a bite myself, assuming I can find something.'

'I've brought some food,' said Abby. 'It's in a cooler in the car. Sit down and let me cook for you.'

There's something I haven't mentioned.

Actually, there's a great deal I haven't mentioned. How could I possibly include everything? Nonetheless, there is something I haven't mentioned which I must have left out on purpose. That's the difference. Or perhaps there isn't any difference. Perhaps I leave out the things I'm not aware of leaving out on purpose. I wonder, too, if my claim that my mind ran on two parallel tracks proved a poor excuse. Doesn't that apply to everyone? Doesn't everyone look back with bewilderment on what they've said and done? Awful things happen, and afterwards you shake your head and would so much like to know why you did one thing rather than another. Why had I never cried? Crying is such an easy signal. It says, Grief! It's that simple. Yet I never cried, not when they could see me. I want to tell the events as they happened, but I can't. At the time, I was convinced that I hadn't cried and that that made me appear insensitive. That was how I saw myself, and it worried me. But I recall now that I did cry, that I cried on several occasions, and that Funder had seen me weeping.

While Abby was in the kitchen, I took a shower and tried to wake myself up. I stood motionless until the water became too hot. I dried my hair with a towel until it frizzed, put on Halland's dressing gown – mine now – and padded back into the living room. My phone and Abby's rang at the same time. I went into the study while Abby fumbled about in the living room looking for her bag. When she retreated to the kitchen, I tried to listen to what she was saying at the same time as I was answering my own call. Funder. He wanted to know if I had found Halland's cell phone. I hadn't even looked. I could hear Abby talking. Did she sound excited? 'Are you there?' asked Funder. Yes, I was there. 'Have you heard about Brandt?' I asked. 'Maybe he's turned up by now, but yesterday he'd gone missing.' 'Are you worried?' Funder asked. 'I'm not sure. He was supposed to have been a pall-bearer at the funeral, so it's a bit strange, don't you think?' 'Yes,' he said. 'It's just that … well, he mentioned something the other day about the Churchyard Committee … have you spoken to them?' 'Do you mean the Parish Council?' 'No … I don't know what he wanted with them. It may have had something to do with Halland …'

The doorbell rang. 'There's someone at the door,' I said cheerfully to Funder. 'It's like a train station here. Let me see who it is.' I hung up.

'I'll get it!' I called to Abby, who stood at the cooker and just nodded. I felt excited. The house had found new life just by her being there: the telephones rang and now we had a visitor.

25

Why so wretched dost thou go
Upon yon troubled way?
Vexed by sorrow and by woe
Anon thou shalt decay!

B. S. Ingemann

I hadn't seen her in years. The first time, I rang the doorbell of my own house and she opened. I wanted to collect Abby, but Abby wouldn't come out and the woman didn't invite me in. I had no idea who she was then. I never liked that house and didn't feel sad when I left it. But there was something about the way she stood in the doorway … I could see myself standing there, too. I had never thought of that doorway as being my place to stand, but then I saw her hand on my doorknob and her long, tanned legs below the hem of her skirt in my hallway. She didn't apologize for Abby not wanting to come out. She was abrupt, standoffish and rather pretty.

And now here she stood in the square outside Halland's house. Not much changed but flustered. Angry, even. 'Is Troels here?' she snapped, stepping forward as if to come in.

I blocked her way without thinking. 'No, he isn't. Why should he be? Anyway, I thought you were divorced. Aren't you?'

'Yes, we bloody well are!' she yelled. 'But it'd be just like him to come here. I've read about that husband of yours.'

'You've read about my husband? How interesting. What do you want? '

'I want to speak to Troels!' I thought she was going to stamp her feet. 'He's been waiting for this to happen for ages!'

'For what to happen?'

Abby appeared behind me. I immediately felt edgy, as though she was a cat that mustn't be let out or else she'd run off and never come back. I tried to stand in the way and she had to peer over my shoulder. 'Hello, Gudrun!' she said. 'What are you doing here?'

Gudrun was aghast. 'No,' she replied, 'what are *you* doing here? You don't even want to be here!'

'Well, she's here anyway,' I trumpeted, only to feel sorry, and then on edge again.

'We're about to have a bite to eat. Do you want to come in?' Abby asked.

'No, she doesn't,' I interrupted as calmly as I could. By now I had realized that I was wearing a dressing gown with my hair in a mess while Gudrun sported a short skirt like last time. She definitely did not want to come in.

'Where are the twins?' asked Abby.

'Oh, kiss my ass!' Gudrun yelled, striding off across the square.

'Kiss it yourself!' we both said. We went back inside.

'Food's ready!' Abby announced. Then the doorbell rang again.

'This time I'm putting some clothes on,' I called, and dashed into the bedroom. 'Don't let her in!'

It wasn't Gudrun, it was a man. Abby let him in; the voices disappeared into the kitchen. I looked at myself in the mirror. The face Gudrun had seen stared back at me. The black shadows under the eyes resulted from lack of sleep, smeared mascara, too much drink and general mortification. My hair was still in a frizz. I had to sort myself out. Perhaps it was Funder who had come around? True, he had only just telephoned, but hadn't said from where.

I had never spent much time on my appearance. My curiosity invariably outweighed my vanity. Nevertheless, I took a while to get ready and when I eventually reappeared in the kitchen I seemed to interrupt an intense conversation. Did Abby's eyes gleam? Brandt's lodger had not yet shaved, so his angular jaw still appeared prominent. His long legs were stretched out in front of him and his hands were folded behind his head. The table was set for three.

He threw me a smile.

'How's your head?' he asked, with a snide look on his face.

'Fine, actually!' I sat down and let Abby serve the food. 'Has Brandt turned up?'

'No. We've reported him missing. I don't know what to say, really ...'

I suddenly imagined the ceiling falling down on our heads. I flinched.

'What's the matter?' asked Abby. I shook my head.

'I hear you were out having a good time last night?' she said.

'I wouldn't call it that,' I replied, glancing across the table at the lodger. I thought that his eyes were blue, but now they shone green. 'I had an awful time, but that's because I was drunk. These things happen. I haven't been drunk in years.'

'That's not true!' said Abby.

I gave her a look. The lodger grinned.

'We haven't seen each other for several years,' I explained. 'This is my daughter.'

'Yes, she told me,' he said. 'The food's lovely!'

'It is. I haven't had anything proper to eat for days,' I said.

'Should I fetch a bottle of wine?' he asked.

'No, thanks.' I went to fill a jug with water. 'I seldom drink at all, and only in small quantities.'

'My parents got divorced because of my mother's drinking!' said Abby, leaning towards the lodger as though they shared some little secret.

I was taken aback. So I said, 'That's not true, Abby, and you know it!'

'Well, I'm glad to hear you've got your drinking under control now!' She continued eating without looking up.

I felt embarrassed. I couldn't really thump the table and declare my sobriety after what had happened the night before, could I? The lodger had seen me dancing with Bjørn, the caretaker, and that's not how I behave when I am sober. Besides, I'd foisted aquavit on him without any rye bread and pickled herring. I decided not to comment. I had no desire to argue with Abby, yet her disdain was palpable.

Although I was looking down at my plate, I couldn't avoid noticing the glances across the table. Not every single one, only the prolonged ones. 'Do you two know each other?' I asked, putting down my knife and fork.

'No. Do we look as if we do?' Abby replied. She almost sparkled.

'Yes, as a matter of fact you do.' I said. The lodger must have been quite a lot older than her. How much older I couldn't say; I was rubbish at guessing people's ages. Anyway, schoolchildren now drove cars and I had a teenager for a bank manager. Pensioners turned out to be my peers. 'What are you actually doing at the museum?'

'Looking at old photographs of the area for my next book,' the lodger said. 'Oh, hell! The bloody dog!'

'Is the dog still at Brandt's? Why hasn't his sister come to collect it?'

'She's in the Canary Islands. Thanks for the dinner. I'm sorry to rush off, but I really must take it for a walk. I only came to tell you about Brandt going missing.'

'Can I come?' said Abby. 'I love dogs! What sort is it?'

I remained seated. 'Will you be coming back?' I called after her. 'Will you be staying the night?' It didn't really matter. I could leave the door on the latch. I wanted to sleep. I felt too exhausted for the Grand Reconciliation. I no longer had the energy to contemplate how that might happen. Perhaps we had already reconciled without my noticing.

26

I feel so poverty-stricken when I see others full of emotional élan.

Karin Michaëlis, *Elsie Lindtner*

Early the next morning, I grabbed my umbrella and walked over to the churchyard. I had woken up with a headache and what I could only call a guilty conscience. I hadn't visited Halland's grave since Friday evening. Was that awful of me? I felt as if I had neglected him but I suspect he couldn't have cared less. It was earlier than I thought, not properly light yet and rather chilly, and the square retained its night-time appearance. The churchyard seemed much quieter than usual, which made my own noise all the more conspicuous. Shadows flitted between the headstones. I wasn't afraid, though I found myself wondering about ghosts. Or was it just the mist? The flowers still lay on Halland's grave, but they had clearly been disturbed, scraped aside at one edge, to expose bare soil. I dutifully contemplated the grave and realized I wouldn't come again. Halland wasn't here. He wasn't even missing, because he had never been here when he was alive. I followed the fjord out of the town, then walked back up to the main street and across the square.

Inger opened her window as I approached the house. Leaning out, she wished me good morning. She approved of my visit to Halland's grave.

'I saw ghosts ...' I said.

Her look shifted to match the one people usually adopted when they took what I said literally.

'There were ghosts flitting about. And someone had disturbed the flowers.'

Inger looked relieved. 'That'll be deer. Don't you remember how they wanted them shot last year? Peter Olsen made such a fuss when they wouldn't let them.' Her expression became distant. We stared at each other.

'Aha,' I said.

'What do you mean, "aha"?'

'Can no one in this town put two and two together?'

'The thought only just occurred to me.'

'What was his name again?'

'Peter Olsen. He's on the Parish Council, or he was. I don't think he is any more.'

'Has he got a hunting licence?'

'I wouldn't know.'

'Would the pastor?'

Inger clutched at her dressing gown and made to close her window. 'For all we know, the police may already have been informed.'

Abby clattered around the kitchen. I smelled coffee and baking.

'Have you made bread?' I asked, aghast.

'You don't mind, do you? It's only one of those packets.'

'Bread is bread!' I said, sitting down in the corner.

'Have you been for a walk?'

'I went to the churchyard.'

'Oh. I'm sorry I haven't said anything about ... him.'

'About what?'

'About your husband dying. Being murdered, I mean. It's so dreadful. I ought to have said something yesterday, but I was feeling so uncertain.'

'You weren't entirely at a loss for words, if I remember correctly. But I wasn't either. I had a hangover and had just escaped from a lunatic. I reeked of pee and puke and needed to sleep. I was just glad to see you after all that time. It didn't matter what you said. Did you sleep upstairs?'

She turned away.

'You're blushing,' I said.

'It was late when I came in. I sneaked upstairs quietly. The bed was made, so I went straight to sleep. Do you want some coffee?'

I did. But first I needed to call Funder. 'Halland may not have been murdered after all. I think he may have been shot by accident by some churchman with a hunting licence.' I told Abby.

Her eyebrows shot up. 'Have some coffee first.'

'You've been mothering me since yesterday,' I said. 'It's as if you're …' I was going to say 'in love,' but I knew the words would make me cry. 'I'll just make that call. Won't be a minute!'

But Funder had already made progress without me. I had alerted him to that line of enquiry the day before, he told me, only without knowing what I was saying. He hadn't spoken to Peter Olsen yet, though. 'I'll get back to you as soon as we've talked to him,' the detective said.

'No need,' I replied, opening my laptop. 'Just call me when you know who did it.'

'Roger,' he said. *Roger?* 'We're trying to get in touch with the woman who put the death notice in the paper. Pernille, wasn't it?'

'She's mad. She knew Halland's sister. I think she went too far putting in that notice. What do you want her for, anyway? She lives in Copenhagen. She's hardly likely to know Peter Olsen.'

'Have you got her surname? Phone number?'

'I'll call you back with the number. Any news about Brandt?'

'I expect you'll know before I do when he comes home,' Funder answered, sounding wounded. 'His car's parked outside the surgery, even though he normally walks there. His secretary can't explain it. On Friday they closed the surgery at noon because of the funeral, but they left separately, and ...'

'And he didn't arrive at the church. I didn't notice who came; I was too embarrassed to look. But I know he wasn't there.'

'Why were you embarrassed?'

'So many people had come because of the notice in the paper.'

The doorbell rang. I heard Abby talking to Brandt's lodger in the hall. Had she made breakfast with him in mind? Craning my neck, I saw her hug him.

'Funder?'

'Yeah?'

'I've found Halland's computer.'

'You did what?'

'I found Halland's computer,' I repeated.

'Where?'

'I've found it, that's all. I don't suppose you'll be needing it once you've got hold of our parish marksman. Assuming he shot Halland by accident, that is.'

'Leave Peter Olsen to me. I'll send someone over to pick up the laptop. But we need to know where you found it!'

I hung up.

'I'll be off, then!' said the lodger as soon as I joined them.

'Not on my account, I hope. Abby's baked a loaf,' I told him.

'Which reminds me, I better take it out of the oven!' she said, squeezing past us with a swing of her hips.

'I've got work to do, I'm afraid,' the lodger explained. 'I just wanted to say ...'

'Goodbye?' I suggested. 'Good morning? Thanks! You were wonderful?'

'Mum!' exclaimed Abby.

They exchanged glances over my head. I was nearly blushing myself now. 'I need the washroom,' I said.

I didn't actually. I stared at my face in the mirror above the sink. I let the water run over my hand, then turned it off. Waited. Peter Olsen. Who was he? And who was that woman in the mirror? That woman's husband is dead. That woman's long-lost daughter has come back. Does it make any difference? Her face is empty, but mirrors always make people's faces look empty. Halland shaved without a mirror. Did I know why he used to do that? Is there no difference at all with him being gone and her being back? *Why* is there no difference? But there *was* a difference. I had a weight on my heart that hadn't been there before Halland died. And I felt a need to laugh that hadn't been there before Abby came back. But my face in the mirror appeared as empty as it always had been.

'Ninety-eight, ninety-nine, a hundred! Coming out, ready or not!' I called.

'He's gone!' she called back.

We sat down in the kitchen again. It was like some kind of unpleasant test, I thought. But the bread tasted good, albeit rather doughy and too hot, right from the oven. I ate and enjoyed, and said nothing. I kept glancing over at Abby. The woman was undoubtedly her. How I could have failed to notice her among ten or twenty other people was beyond me. These were the same brown eyes, the same blonde hair, though darker and she wore it up now. She had put on a bit of weight and resembled Troels's sister just as she had done as a child. But she looked like me too. I could see myself in her. And I was happy. Then I felt ashamed to be happy.

'I didn't open them or anything,' she said. 'But I found some boxes on the shelf upstairs ... they had my name on them.'

'You may open them if you want. They're for you.'

'What's in them?'

I took a deep breath. 'All sorts of things I was going to tell you about.'

'What do you mean?'

'They're full of notebooks. Not diaries, because I don't keep one, but ... well, there were so many things I needed to tell you. You were growing up, you didn't want to see me, so I wrote to you instead.'

'I'm sorry,' said my daughter, 'but this all sounds a bit weird, if you ask me.'

I cringed. I had never imagined she could think like that. The notebooks were meant for Abby the child.

'I suppose it is, in a way,' I said. 'I haven't been well since ... no, that's not what I mean. Actually, I don't know what I mean. Don't read any of them. They will only embarrass us both. We don't know each other any more. I intended those notebooks for the person you were then ...'

'Give me an example.'

I thought for a moment. 'For example, I wrote about how I thought I was having an erotic experience when all I was doing was kissing a door.'

'Mum!'

'It's true. I was having a sleepover with some friends. This was when I was a teenager – the last throes. I was nineteen, I think. And there I was on the floor, kissing this boy I had a crush on. Kissing what I thought was his upper arm.'

'But it was a door?'

'No, it was my sleeping bag. It had this shine, like the skin on a young man's upper arm.'

'Oh, come off it!'

'I imagined that was the kind of thing one told one's daughter as she was growing up. So I wrote it down.'

'But there's boxes and boxes ...' She gestured despondently in the direction of the stairs. She was right, no one, not even I, would read all that rubbish.

'Do you know about Martin Guerre?' I asked. 'He's rolled up in Halland's study. I don't have a big enough wall.'

'What do you mean?'

'Martin Guerre deserted his family and his village. Then along came someone called Arnaud du Tilh, pretending to be Martin Guerre. He had everyone fooled, even Martin Guerre's wife. So the story goes.'

'What are you talking about?'

'Do you recognize me?'

'How do you mean?'

'Do you recognize me? Do I talk like your mother did when you were a child? Am I more human now, or still a monster? Or the other way round? What am I? Can you tell me who I am?'

For a moment she didn't respond. 'You're a bit dippy,' she said.

'And you're in love,' I said. 'Lucky thing.'

27

(The doorbell rings)
MR. SMITH: *Goodness, someone is ringing.*
MRS. SMITH: *There must be someone there. I'll go and see.*

Eugène Ionesco, *The Bald Soprano*

My grandfather was dead. I didn't cry. Abby was still with me when my mother rang to tell her. My mother didn't call me, but I knew. She was probably offended that I hadn't told her the date of Halland's funeral. She loved a tit-for-tat: one funeral for another. Abby said she would go with me, but I wasn't upset. I could do without seeing my mother. Anyway I had stopped missing my grandfather after I had spoken to him on the phone. He had been kind to me as a child. But the moment he called me 'dear' three times in two minutes I remembered that he was a miserable, resentful old man nonetheless. The funeral was arranged for the Monday, but I couldn't attend. I was suppose to give a talk at a library in Jutland that Sunday and would be hard pressed to arrive in Reading on time. At least that's what I told myself. Telling the talk's organizer that my husband had died was out of the question, and I didn't want to use my grandfather as an excuse either. So I should just go to Jutland as planned, thereby avoiding having to involve a stranger in my private life. I had already been on the front page of one of the tabloids, but the headline merely said, WRITER IN MOURNING. I could have been anyone; and anyway, Pernille appeared more prominently in the photo.

Abby asked who she was. 'Is that the kind of paper you read?' I returned her question.

I had given Halland's laptop to Funder, though I still hadn't told the police about the rented room. But they are very clever. Pernille rang on the Wednesday morning to say that they were standing outside her door and wanted to see Halland's room. 'Let them in,' I said. 'They've got the key.'

Boarding the train to Jutland felt like a relief. I just grabbed my bag, the one Halland had taught me always to have at the ready. On the train, I plugged my cell phone in to charge and busied myself with the quick crossword, trying not to think. TWINGE—CONTRACTION, EXCLAMATION—ALAS, HOLLOW—TROUGH, DIVIDE—HALVE, MALE—BUCK.

I had received a text. From my editor, one of the few people who had the number. He couldn't get through on the landline; would I call him? He had written the text the day Halland died. I deleted it.

Although I had never met the man who organized my reading, I could tell that he knew about my husband's murder. But he said nothing, and as we drove from the station to the new library I wondered whether I should be offended by his lack of manners. Ought he not to offer his condolences, at the very least mention that he had read the awful news in the paper or heard an announcement on the radio? But truth to tell, I wasn't offended. I wouldn't have known how to react anyway if he had mentioned Halland.

'I've been pushing for you to be our writer of the month!' the man told me, blinking three times in quick succession.

'Thank you.'

'Have you decided what you're going to read?'

'Not yet. I like to get a feel of the audience first.'

'I hope the turnout will be all right. On a sunny day like today, a lot of people will want to be out in their gardens. Do you take requests?'

'I suppose so.'

'You might not think it suitable, but you published a story in a journal about ten years ago. None of your books include the piece, but I think it is magnificent. I brought a copy along in case you'd like to read it.'

'Sounds intriguing.'

When he unlocked the library door, I noticed a large poster for another event three days earlier. He traced my gaze.

'Yes, that was one of the library's own events. We're only a small group, so we borrow a room in the basement.'

The building was lovely, though. Filled with light from the bright sun. He locked the door behind us.

'How will people get in?' I gestured towards the locked door.

'The library's closed,' he said. 'But I will send Birthe up to stand by the door. She's downstairs preparing the coffee, I should think.' I sighed. I knew the routine. He ushered me into a small office where I sat down in a deep armchair. He left me alone. I heard them discuss how many people might come and how much coffee they needed to make. Birthe came in, said hello and handed me a fat envelope and a form to fill in. 'Might as well do it now,' she said, 'so you have a fighting chance to catch the train after the reading.'

'Shouldn't you be guarding the door?' I asked.

'Someone else is doing that,' she replied. 'Two people have already arrived.'

I knew the scenario off by heart. The organizer came back into the room and handed me a photocopy of my old story. Without looking at it, I filled in the form with my ID number and address, and peeked inside the envelope. Seeing my fee in cash livened me up. Putting the form on the table, I stuffed the photocopy and the envelope in my bag and stood up. The organizer looked flustered as I strode past him.

'I don't understand,' he said. 'We usually get about twenty-five people.'

'I'm just popping out for some air,' I said.

'You mean a smoke?'

'No, some air.'

He gestured down the corridor towards a glass door.

'That's an exit. Just make sure to leave the lock on the latch so you can get back in again.'

I let the door slam behind me, went up some steps and found myself at the rear of the building. I gazed on lawns, sculptures, shade. A gravel path led into what looked like a small park.

Walking briskly, I glanced back over my shoulder like a thief, then ran, faster and faster, past old people on benches, past a play area and a fountain. When I reached the pedestrianized area I ambled along like a tourist. The shops were shut except for a pizzeria with tables on the pavement. When I asked the way to the railway station, I was annoyed with myself for saying *railway* station. People always gave me funny looks when I used that expression. I was hungry but I only wanted to go home. The next train was due in fifteen minutes. I walked through the tunnel beneath the tracks to the opposite platform and stood in the sun. I felt liberated, which was a much better feeling than having completed a task. After finishing a job, I always worry that I could have done better. But now, I only felt relieved to be on my way home.

My phone chimed and I searched around in my bag.

One new message, it said. I pressed DISPLAY. The message was from Halland.

28

Third no return address. I cannot answer. He wants no
answer. What does he want?

Anne Carson, *The Beauty of the Husband*

'Funder! Funder, Funder, Funder,' I repeated to myself. I was
so worked up that I pressed the wrong keys. The text disappeared. What did it say? When the train arrived, I hesitated but
eventually decided to board. I found a window seat, dumped
my jacket and went out into the vestibule with my phone. I
realized I didn't have Funder's number and I couldn't call the
emergency services because there was no emergency. What did
the text say? I tried to remain calm and methodical. I clicked
on my inbox. There was only one message and it was from
Halland. I pressed the OPEN key. *Where are you?* it said. 'No,
please, please, please,' I repeated, shaking my head vigorously.
'That's not funny. That's not funny!' Soldiers came through the
carriage and one of them asked if I was all right. He had such
a kind voice I could hardly bear it. 'No,' I said. 'Yes, I mean.'
He scrutinized me for a moment. I nodded. 'Everything's fine,'
I said, repeating the words after the soldiers carried on through
the carriage. Everything's fine.

The conductor came through and asked for the ticket. I
fumbled with my bag, then with my purse and my phone. 'Is
the reception especially poor around here?' I asked. 'I need to
make a call, but I can't get a signal!'

'It's always weak around here,' she replied.

'But I need to make a call!' I repeated, my voice rising.

'Is something wrong?'

I bit my tongue. This shouldn't have happened. Shaking my head, I peered into my bag so the conductor wouldn't see my face. I tasted blood in my mouth.

My jacket still lay on my seat when I got back. A man sitting on the aisle seat was reading a fat crime novel. He got up laboriously while I waited impatiently, fidgeting as if in a hurry. Across the table from us sat two women and our legs had to find space to settle. I took out my newspaper, all the while gripping my phone. I had finished the quick crossword on the outward journey. Now I began to read. We were still burdened with the same omniscient, incompetent government. There were still forgotten wars in Africa. We continued to wage war on terrorism: everyone was under surveillance; everything had to be dragged out into the light; soon there would be no secrets any more. I hadn't paid attention to the newspapers' take on my own story and found myself gazing at Halland's picture for a while before I recognized him.

Keeping my eye on the signal bars on my phone, I read about Peter Olsen. Apparently the police had spoken to him and concluded that he could not have shot Halland. He had an alibi. He had spent the night at his sister's in Kalvehave. He had driven home only after breakfast; Halland was already dead by then. The police were running tests on Olsen's hunting rifle. I looked out of the window. The sun was still shining, but the light seemed odd; perhaps because of the tinted glass. Poppies appeared in the yellow sky. Maybe I was looking at a poppy field? During my childhood lots of poppies used to grow in fields and on building sites. Then they disappeared for years. Now they had returned.

The train came to a stop. The passengers glanced at each other in annoyance. They raised their eyebrows and sighed.

'Are we running late?' I asked the man next to me.

'They just said we'll be moving in a minute.'

I looked at my phone again. Pressed the number for directory enquiries. No connection. I felt a hot flash and shifted uneasily in my seat. Why did I get hot flashes now?

'Do you want to get out?' the man asked.

I shook my head, gasping a bit, then closed my eyes and tried to think of nothing.

'The same thing happened the last time I took the train,' he said. 'Stuck for two hours we were. What a palaver. Can't open the windows or doors ... the recycled air is awful.'

Were they really unable to open the doors? Another hot flash. I couldn't breathe any longer. Can one forget how to breathe? I wanted to get out. I thought I said so, but the man didn't seem to have heard me. Who had Halland's phone? I could play along and reply as though he were still alive. The loudspeaker crackled. We would be sitting here indefinitely, they couldn't find the fault. The man looked at his watch.

'I'll miss my bus,' he said.

'And I need to make a call,' I said, barely breathing. My mouth was parched.

'That time last winter, all we could do was sit and wait. No information at all, then all the lights went out. Pitch black it was. We all had to walk back along the tracks to Vejle.'

'So they *can* open the doors,' I said, breathing more easily at the thought.

'Only in emergencies. Highly dangerous business sending folk out onto the tracks.'

I rested my cheek against the windowpane and relished the brief chill, pressing my face hard against the glass, moving my lips across it. Could I taste anything? The glass tasted of metal. Soft, soft, dark.

Soft, dark.

I mustn't make the taste sound luscious. I was frightened, really frightened. I have tried to come to terms with my physical self since I was born, just as I assume everyone else has with greater or lesser success. Anyway, you get to know your physical self and every now and then even gain a fleeting sense of pleasure from some part of your body. I had had my ups and downs. But this feeling was new. Perhaps I had never been frightened before. Of course I had felt fear when Halland was lying there. But then I didn't think anything much because I didn't know what was happening. Now my body expressed what I felt and I had no say in the matter. A paranoid itch between the shoulder blades on a bathing jetty was nothing compared to this. I fainted. Or rather, I had a blackout; I think that's what they would call it. A second or two, perhaps, maybe more. I slumped against the man in the aisle seat. He nudged me; his moustache nearly touched my face.

'I want to get out,' I said.

'They won't let you.'

'I want to get out. I really *must* make that call. It's urgent.'

'You've got claustrophobia. I'm having trouble breathing myself.'

'I want to get out!' Sitting up, I swivelled my head gingerly, then tried to stand up. The man remained seated. As I stepped over his legs, I straddled him for a moment before he grabbed me. 'Let go!' I said. Everyone stared. I wanted to sit down again and be quiet and ordinary, but too late.

Suddenly we jerked into motion. I banged my chin against the man's head. His breath smelt of eggs. I found my feet, then lost my balance and fell towards the aisle. My phone chimed again as the floor reared up. I stayed on the floor and opened the message. It was from Halland: *Where are you?* I rang his number, still on the floor, breathing heavily. The phone rang. I imagined him in the car, perhaps in the narrow bed with Pernille, staring up at the poster of Martin Guerre that hung like an altarpiece above his head, in the living room at home, at the window with his binoculars. No answer.

29

'...but I cannot credit it until I see it with my own eyes.'
Arabian Nights

Funder told me to stay calm and think things through. He wasn't as shocked as I. I regained control of my breathing and switched off the phone. I drove home from the station intent on my driving. I didn't sing. I felt dead inside, as though swaddled in cotton wool. The rational part of me knew that I wasn't dying, that Halland was dead and that whoever had sent me the text messages had not been Halland. The cotton-wool feeling changed into a burning sensation. With the heat I became weightless and short of breath. But I drove home fully focused, although I felt I occupied a no-man's-land and didn't really exist.

I have no idea how my brain works. Every few years I used to write a collection of stories. That was what I did. How they came about I no longer know. I read a lot and went for long walks. I was often on my own because Halland travelled a lot. Sometimes we went away together, though never when he was working. I lived mostly on his money, though I seldom gave such matters much thought. Not even now. I sat in the car on the square, feeling too heavy to get out and go into the house. Brandt's house was dark and so was mine.

Finding my phone in my bag, I turned it on again, holding my breath. Nothing more from Halland. Six unanswered calls from the ever-alert detective, and one text: *Don't turn off your phone. Call us immediately if that number contacts you again.* That number.

Funder was so very correct. And tanned. I rang Brandt. No one picked up. His house was dark. Where was he? Where was the lodger? Abby was in England. Halland was in the churchyard. I turned off the phone, then took out of my bag the envelope of cash and the photocopy. I opened the car door, so that the automatic light inside the car came on. I peered at the story title, then at the first page. 'Wondrous Derailment.' I remembered it now. The uncoupling. That was me.

'Oh dear!' I exclaimed.

Now I had said 'Oh dear' several times. It couldn't go on. It wasn't enough. I couldn't just sit here. I had to do something. Buy a pet. Or sell up and move on. Yes, sell up and move on. No, buy a pet – a grey cat. But I couldn't stand animals. And I was fond of the house, so why should I leave?

I just wanted to lie on the sofa and watch TV. Please don't think I never watched television. Now things were back to normal and I could finally switch it on again. All I needed for happiness was a detective series. And there were lots to choose from. Simplicity was a virtue. First a murder, nothing too bestial. Then a police inspector. Insights into his or her personal problems, perhaps. Details about the victim. Puzzles and anomalies. Lines of investigation. Clues. Detours. Breakthrough. Case solved. Nothing like real life. I watched one thriller, then another. But as soon as the penny dropped, I lost interest. The puzzle attracted me – the solution left me cold. Nothing like real life. When only the loose ends were left to tie up, I usually went into the kitchen to fetch something to eat, or went to the washroom. But when I got back, the police inspector had almost invariably realized, at the last minute, that the amicable individual in whom he had been confiding was in fact the villain. In the twinkling of an eye, someone found themselves in grave danger. Their rescue involved a few last-gasp killings before the villain was allowed to explain his sick, jealous mind or the abuse he had suffered as a child. Nothing like real life. The plot might have started off plausibly, but then all similarity disappeared. And another thing: this crime thriller appeared far better organized and far more real than my own life.

I decided to make a list to focus my thoughts. Perhaps we could all gather in the drawing room at the end, when the detective had worked it out. Leaning back on the sofa with a notepad on my knee, I chewed on a pen as the opening credits of the next detective thriller scrolled across the screen.

Halland (dead)
Shot
Deer
Peter Olsen (rifle)
Pernille (apartment, redirected mail)
Stine (in the woods)
Brandt (missing)

I was none the wiser, unable even to organize those few points. On the back of the sheet of paper I wrote:

Laundry
Groceries
Dry cleaning
~~Go through~~
Letters
Room at P

As I settled myself more comfortably, my body remembered the morning when I had gone to sleep here not long before Halland was shot. With an unfamiliar sense of satisfaction I had imagined myself reading to him what I had written the previous night. I hadn't shown him my work for a long time, although in earlier days I often read it out loud to him, sitting on the kitchen counter while he cooked. He took pleasure in this routine, I think; sometimes he laughed. Now, just when I had finally made a start on a new book, he had to die. I was angry. My anger was of course unwarranted, but far worse was my desire for revenge. Not towards the murderer – the gunman was too abstract to inspire feeling. Rather, I wanted to kill Halland myself. Was that because of his secrets or because his death was preventing me from finishing the book?

In my life I often thirsted for revenge, though I never managed to satisfy my thirst to the extent my grandfather once did. As an adult I came to suspect that he had stolen the tale from someone else, but as a child I couldn't hear it enough. My grandfather was a difficult child and badly behaved at school. His teacher would beat him with a cane and with his bare hands. No one ever intervened; there was no law against caning. Years later, when my grandfather was twenty-three and had turned into a broad-shouldered bricklayer, he met his former teacher in the street. The teacher greeted him with enthusiasm – a detail that added significantly to the listener's craving for retribution: the man was completely unaware of the wrongs he had committed! Like a fool, he invited my grandfather home for tea. There, to get his own back, my grandfather beat the living daylights out of him.

I wanted to hear the story over and over again. And yet I never had the courage to ask what the teacher looked like by the time Grandfather had finished with him. Was he bleeding? Lying crumpled on the floor? Sobbing? Were his bones broken? Did he die? None of that seemed relevant. The sense of retribution was the shocking element. I could picture the terror in the teacher's eyes. But to whom was I to administer a beating now?

My gaze fell on the windowsill facing the garden. Halland's binoculars stood on top of his bird book, a heavy, rather dog-eared volume. I knew that he annotated the pages, scribbled little symbols to indicate that he had observed this or that bird, as well as locations, dates and sometimes a commentary on song or behaviour. I had listened when he told me about a particular bird and followed his gestures when he pointed one out. In time, I learnt to spot a few raptors. I could tell the difference between a black-headed gull and a tern, and was familiar with winter plumage. I listened to him mainly at the beginning of our relationship. I retrieved the book and returned to the sofa. A piece of paper fell out from between the pages. Halland's handwriting. *Apus apus*, it said. *The common swift spends almost its entire life in flight. Food and nesting materials are collected on the wing. Drinking, bathing, even sleep too. Normally, a swift will interrupt flight only for the purpose of breeding. When young leave the nest they often remain airborne for three years until returning to breed. ME.*

ME? What did that mean? I read the words out loud, thinking they sounded like poetry that might fill a person with both joy and sorrow. But Halland was no poet, and what he had written was merely fact. *ME?* 'Oh, stop it!' I burst out. 'Just stop it, will you!'

30

'Cleaning merely stirs up the dust. Leave well alone and the dust stays where it is.'

Edvard Munch, according to Rolf E. Stenersen

Monday. Good! Were we finally back to normal? You could argue I had been away on business in Jutland. I didn't cope very well, but now I was getting there.

If normal weekday life had resumed, the washing needed attention. I filled the machine. I toyed with the idea of going for a walk, buying some groceries and then sitting down to write. Instead, I made some coffee and went upstairs. Martin Guerre was still rolled up in Halland's study. I had put the redirected mail on his desk. It had been preying on my mind. I tore open the envelopes and pulled out the contents. Placing the letters in a pile, I read them one by one, counted them, then went through them again. Reminders. All of them. One said our telephone was going to be cut off. I went downstairs, lifted the receiver and found that the line was dead. Did they have to do that now?

I knew everything about Halland. He was the love of my life. Did I hate him? As I pulled a sweater over my head and crossed the square, I felt that I did. I entered the bank on the high street and went straight through to the desks behind the counter, where Kirsten was sitting. She stood up to greet me and then, gently holding my elbow, ushered me into a room at the back.

'Have you closed Halland's account? That's what happens, isn't it, when people die? I have no money of my own. Why didn't anyone tell me?'

One thing at a time. Kirsten poured me some coffee. Looking over at me, she said, 'Now, tell me what's the matter.'

'Our phone's been cut off!'

'Things never happen that fast. What's Halland's ID number?'

I gave her his number. She stared at a computer screen, then looked back across the desk at me. 'It seems that Halland cancelled his standing orders some time ago. Are they now supposed to come out of your account?'

'That wouldn't make any sense. I hardly use my account, there's so little money in it.' I gave Kirsten my own ID number.

'Well,' she said, 'there's 2,700 in your current account. And in your interest-bearing account ...'

'That's to pay my taxes ...'

'Is there supposed to be more than half a million?'

'How much?'

Nodding, she clicked on the mouse a few more times.

'Where's it all from?'

'From Halland. He transferred a large sum about a month ago, 450,000 kroner. Were you not aware of that?'

Was I aware of that? I stood up and walked out past the cashiers onto the high street.

'If that number should contact you again,' Funder had written. I had been contacted. What a lot of money!

Back in my living room, I simply yelled, 'What's going on?' Halland couldn't possibly have known that he was going to die, and neither would he have *wanted* to die. He had battled to survive his illness. On the other hand, he had clearly developed some sort of scheme, something he had been close to achieving.

He had moved his papers out of the house. He had transferred bags of money into my account. That must be illegal. What would I want with all that money? I needed to pay the bills, but what else? I could only think of one explanation. He wanted to leave me. But that made no sense. The house was his. Was there another woman? That lunatic in the woods? Pernille? I went to my desk, rummaged for the note with her number on it, then sat with the receiver to my ear before remembering that the line was dead.

Had I stopped to think, I would have taken the car. But I wasn't thinking. Climbing on my bike, I cycled towards the woods through the wind and rain. Laburnum. Lilac. Drizzle. I needed the rhythm of words to penetrate the headwind. Whoever had planted that hedgerow with laburnum and lilac should've been given a medal, assuming they were still alive. Which was unlikely.

Stine was in. Sitting down on the bench at the side of her house to get my breath back, I realized that she played the piano better than most lunatics, if that was her playing inside. I listened for a bit. When the piece came to an end, I went round to the front door. Through the little round pane I saw a pair of feet. Was she standing on her head? I lifted my hand, ready to knock, but my nerves failed me. If Halland had been planning to move in with Stine, I didn't want to know. I crept away from the door, grabbed my bike and walked slowly back along the path. The rain had stopped. I didn't feel like going home. What were those birds sitting on the telephone line? Were they swallows? Were they swifts? No. They were perched in a row, not in the air. Was Halland a swift, living on the wing, never landing? I had no idea how to analyze poetry, only how to enjoy it. Specialist litera-ture was a mystery to me too. I interpreted words at face value.

Normally, a swift will interrupt flight only for the purpose of breeding. In my mind's eye, I saw Halland dancing in the garden. 'Come out, come out!' he had called. Did I go to him?

When I arrived back in the square, Bjørn the caretaker was walking towards his car. He raised his hand in greeting. I raised mine, then waved to indicate that I wanted to speak to him. He came over. He looked embarrassed. I gripped the handlebars of my bike.

'What exactly did you hear Halland say?' I asked.

He took a deep breath and thought for a moment. 'My wife has killed me.'

'But he can't have said that, surely? Are you quite certain?'

He furrowed his brow. 'Yes. At least I think so.'

'Is that what you told the police?'

'As far as I remember.'

I felt annoyed. 'That's not the sort of thing you should say without being certain!'

'Well, it's a while ago now,' he protested. 'I'm fairly sure that's what I told them.'

Shaking my head, I walked my bike towards the gate. 'Do you fancy dinner at the Postgården?' he called after me.

'I always eat there on Mondays,' Bjørn the caretaker said as we walked down the hill together. I never had supper at the Postgården. In fact, it was a long time since I had done anything as unremarkable as walking down the hill to the Postgården.

The dish of the day was a traditional fatty roast pork with potatoes and gravy. We waited in silence for the food to come. When it arrived, I fell on it. Eventually I looked up. The caretaker pointed at my plate and said, 'You've eaten everything!' He had removed the fat from his pork and left a large potato. 'I was hungry,' I replied, getting up to go to the washroom. Was I going to throw up again? I had forgotten to check if there were any traces of my previous mishap on Stine's step. Cold sweat appeared on my forehead. I was back in the woods. How had I got there that night? What about my bike? Stine didn't have a car. Didn't I see a car? My editor once scribbled a note on the side of one of my manuscripts. Halland would tease me about it: *Are there going to be any more flashbacks?* I hardly knew what flashbacks were any more. My life was a continuous stream of flashbacks. Like now: I went to the ladies. I read the words on the toilet-paper dispenser: *TORK*. And immediately all the other times I had sat in a cubicle in the ladies' washroom recalling Thorkild Hansen's French nickname, *Mon Tork*, came back to me. I had repeated the word to myself in many a public convenience. Flashbacks were all that was left.

When I returned to the table, Bjørn had gone. 'He paid the bill,' Betina said from across the room. 'Would you like some coffee?' Nodding, I sat down at my empty plate. I saw people at the harbour, near the side entrance of the old warehouse. The view reminded me of something I was supposed to remember but had forgotten. Had I killed Halland? Was that even plausible? Had he really said that I had? I hadn't shot him, I knew that much. I couldn't even hit a barn door that time I tried to apply for a hunting licence in my youth.

'I didn't have a chance to talk to him,' I said when Betina put a cup of coffee in front of me.

'It's nice to see you getting out again,' she said. 'How are you?'

Why was she so friendly? I had come here a few times for coffee, but we had never exchanged more than two words. I almost told her I was fine, but I didn't. Partly because it wasn't true, partly because it would be the wrong thing to say. So all I did was shrug.

'Well, it's no wonder!' she said.

I never found that the words people said to each other revealed to any great extent what happened between them. A single word never changed anything. A word was not an illumination that lodged itself in the brain and led a person to find a murderer. A word could never wound someone fatally. Love couldn't die on account of a mere word. One word would always be followed by another that compounded or expounded, repaired or derailed. Not even that second word would be decisive. Not in a good way, at any rate. There were times when I lost the inclination to speak. Silence felt simple and straight-forward – but also indicated a lack. Silence acted on a person like a prison or a cramped cell. My mother had the ability to repeat my words in such a way that I both recognized myself and realized that she had completely misunderstood. 'But you said you were afraid of him!' she once claimed, referring to a former teacher of mine. Her voice was high-pitched, almost triumphant. She wiped her lips with a napkin. It wouldn't have helped if I had retold the story more accurately or slanted it differently. She drew her own conclusions. That's just one example. Other people behaved just like her. Me too. I wasn't any different.

As soon as I got home, I rang Pernille on my cell phone. Halland's jacket was still on the peg in the hall. At first she expressed reluctance. 'I've already told you,' she said.

'But he was having his mail redirected!'

'I've no idea why he did that.'

'Why didn't you ever come to see us?'

'I don't know. I suppose I never needed to, not with him coming here so often. You sound so angry. It can't be my fault, surely?'

'Why did he want to be present at the birth of your baby?'

'He offered to be there, that's all. Perhaps because he didn't have any children. How should I know? Perhaps he just wanted to see a baby being born. I appreciated the offer, since I had no one else to turn to.'

'Oh, what rubbish!' I barked, and hung up.

What now? A book to read. Find a book. Wolf, maybe. Something melancholy and meditative. Something beautiful. Lying down on the sofa, I turned to page 47. *The rest is silence. Yet again, I realized that our lives take place inside our minds.* I felt better already. My hands stopped shaking.

31

'*Say something, Pierrot!*'

Children at the Tivoli Gardens

Afterwards. Of course, afterwards you always know what you should have said. I went barging into Inger's house without realizing that the electricity was off there too. I made straight for the sound of her voice. Four candles burned in a holder in the kitchen. The man sitting opposite Inger was Brandt. I flung myself at him, almost going down on my knees, my hands clutching wherever they could get a grip. He didn't get up.

'Brandt!' I shouted out, only to remember immediately that he had said, 'Can't you stop calling me Brandt now that Halland's dead?' We must have been sitting in a car when he said that. When could that have been? But everyone called him Brandt, even Inger.

I didn't say, 'Where have you been?' or 'Are you all right?' or 'What happened to you?' Instead I started wailing, 'Why? Why did he have to die? It doesn't make sense. You remember how ill he was!' Slumping across Brandt's knee, I wept. It took me a while before I realized that he wasn't responding. Gripping my shoulders, Inger persuaded me to stand up. 'Be gentle. He's only just arrived. He hasn't said a thing. Come and sit down.'

The three of us sat in the flickering light, staring into each other's shadowy faces. I studied Brandt's unshaven skin. He didn't return my gaze. Now the real questions began to surface. I wanted to ask them. But then I suddenly remembered that I hadn't locked my door. The candle wax was dripping. There was a draft. Had I forgotten to shut Inger's door? Had I shut my own? I should check.

'When did you get back? Where have you been?' I asked Brandt. He didn't reply.

'Have you rung the police?'

Brandt turned his head. 'That despicable man ...' he muttered.

'What man?'

Raising his hand, he pointed at me. 'Why didn't you come?'

'Where to?'

'You promised!'

'Promised what?'

'Down there.' He stared straight past me. He spoke with great effort.

'He told you ... to go down there!'

'What's he talking about? Down where?' I asked Inger, then looked back at Brandt. 'I don't understand.'

'Despicable!' he said.

'Who is?'

'I want to go home!'

Inger stood up and peered out of the window. 'I'll take you home when the power comes back on.'

'That's why I'm here,' I said. 'I thought they'd turned off the electricity because we hadn't paid. I may have left the door open. Let me pop back and see.' I wanted to be on my own. Brandt was acting so oddly and I didn't understand what he was saying. He looked at me. 'I don't understand what you are talking about,' I said.

32

In favorem tertii: in favour of a third party

Legal term

The front door is ajar.

I push it open. Something comes hurtling out and nearly knocks me over. It lets out a yelp and makes off past Brandt's house. A dog. The power still hasn't come on. 'Is anyone there?' I call out. Why should anyone be there? Is there a monster in the darkness?

'What are you doing?' I ask. A dark figure is sitting in a corner on the floor. He clears his throat.

'Abby says … you don't seem to be grieving.'

'Does she indeed?'

'Says you're flitting about, drinking and dancing. Flirting, and kissing the neighbour.'

'That's not what Abby says at all.'

'You're drinking again.'

'I don't drink.'

'You're not grieving.'

'Abby wouldn't know.'

'Are you grieving?'

'What's it to you?'

I attack the monster. We roll around on the floor. He is on top, I'm underneath, then we switch places. The windows are illuminated by the white summer night, but on the living-room floor we are in darkness. I catch a glimpse of the bridge of his

137

nose. He doesn't look familiar. He's hurting me. Are we fighting? 'Oh!' I exclaim. My index finger brushes the back of his neck and I'm no longer in doubt. I know who he is now. I'm not afraid. I'm not dreaming. I'll need to pull myself together in a moment. Then I'm hugging him from behind, unable to tell if he is asleep. I awake with him crawling across my face. I pretend to be sleeping. He is standing at the window. The sky gives out its pale light, though it is still night. He snuggles back down with me, top to tail. What's he up to? Taking hold of my foot, he tries to open his mouth wide enough to take the heel between his lips. That is how we lie, my heel in his mouth, me pretending to be asleep. What does he want, I ask myself. 'Leave,' I whisper. '*It's better to have loved and lost, than never to have loved at all.*' His voices trembles as he scrutinizes me. 'Oh, stop it,' I say. 'Go home.' 'But I've waited all this time.' 'For what?' 'For you.' 'What a shame,' I tell him.

33

As gently as possible, she prepared her brother for the duty he must soon perform. Charles then asked for a day off work, she packed her straitjacket and together they went to the asylum where he would leave her until she recovered.

Kathy Watson, *The Devil Kissed Her:*
The Story of Mary Lamb

I went outside with the washing. Across the cold floor of the utility room and out onto the wet grass. The sun blazed on the blue fjord. Everything looked so clear, though nothing was. I hung the sheets on the line. A gentle breeze tugged at them. Early that morning, I made a start on a short story. A single page, that was all. Now I heard Inger's voice. My name. The detective. They hadn't seen me. I pulled down on the clothes line and surveyed them from behind the sheets. Inger's hair was streaked with grey and tousled. That surprised me. Funder looked round-shouldered. He wore a shirt as green as fire – if fire could be green. 'Hey!' I called. They came towards me. They were talking about Brandt.

'Where is he?' I asked.

'At home, asleep. His lodger's gone, so he's on his own,' said Inger. 'All of a sudden, there he was. Out there on the bench, last night. Goodness knows where he's been. I don't think he's well.'

Of course he wasn't well.

'He's been held captive,' I said.

Funder pushed his sunglasses onto the top of his head, narrowed his eyes against the sun. 'How do you know that?'

'Down at the harbour, in the old warehouse,' I said.

'First you know nothing, then you know everything.'

'It was because I kissed him.'

Funder shook his head.

'You kissed Brandt?'

'I can explain.'

He raised a finger. 'I'll be over in a minute,' he said.

'Good,' I said.

Troels lay on the sofa. I handed him a cup of coffee and sat down. 'How can anyone be so jealous at your age, and for what?' I asked him. 'You must have lost your mind. You do realize you could go to jail?'

He said nothing.

'Where are you staying anyway?'

'I'm sleeping in the warehouse. I bought it.'

'You *bought* it?'

'Yes.'

'I thought I was over you, but I know you too well,' I said. The muscle of his cheek twitched. 'I lay in bed with my laptop this morning and wrote the first page of a story about you. I'm calling it "The Clerk."'

'Is that what I am?'

'In your own way. Stay there and I'll read to you.'

Cheek trembling, he closed his eyes. I read:

> It looked as if someone had committed a murder on that bed. Before leaving the tiny room, I leaned against the door frame and contemplated the sheet. A piece of evidence, soiled with blood and excrement. Then came a creeping sense of satisfaction.

*Outside, snow fell. The solicitor made his way gingerly over the
icy flags from next door. He gave a shudder and failed to notice
when I waved to him through the window. If only he knew. That
the clerk had forced open the little window that night. That he
had frightened the life out of Miss Jensen and given it back to me.*

*The clerk was a young man of vigour. Stark naked and
smeared with blood, he had staggered out into the hallway in
the night to find a shower and had found Miss Jensen instead.
Miss Jensen with her weak heart. I lay in the bloodbath and considered his distinguished profile in the half-light, chewing at a
corner of the duvet, weeping as I laughed. I shall never forget her
scream. Or his bashfully energetic presence when he returned
wet and clean to the bed. He has no idea who I am. It puzzles
me rather that he doesn't want to know. On the other hand, I
know best how little there is to know, and refrain from making
a spectacle of myself.*

I giggled.

Troels turned and gave me a wounded look. 'The story does not
come across as the work of a grieving widow. More like that of a
teenager, if you ask me. Abby's right. You're not grieving at all.'

'That's something else entirely.'

'It's not even about me.'

'Yes, it is. Metaphorically. About the time when I knew you,
when you were young and happy.'

'That's a long time ago.'

'Yes.'

'Perhaps the story is more about you than me.'

'No. It's about you.'

The doorbell rang. 'Goodness!' I said, and jumped to my feet.
'That'll be the police.'

34

So there I was, wondering why old Handel or his scriptwriter couldn't say a thing once and let it go at that. Every line in The Messiah *seemed to be repeated again and again.*

John Mortimer, *Rumpole and the Brave New World*

Wednesday morning.

The sparrows chirped.

I had forgotten to take the sheets in and now they were damp with dew. Brandt sat in his wicker chair with a blanket around him.

'Hello!' I said, as kindly as I could, and stepped through the gap in the hedge. 'Feeling any better?' Shrugging, he pursed his lips as though tasting something bitter. 'I'm so sorry,' I said. I put my hand against his cheek. He recoiled slightly, but then leaned into my palm with a sigh.

'My daughter came to see me!'

'Did she?' His face brightened.

'She was quite taken with your lodger!'

Nodding, he looked past me. 'But was she taken with *you?*'

A good question.

'She sent me a postcard.'

'Well, I never!' He sounded like an old woman.

'My cousin doesn't want to know me any more. She wrote to me too – a whole letter. I forgot to tell her about Halland's funeral, so now she wants nothing to do with me.'

'How could you forget to tell your only female friend?'

'She says I think only about myself.'

'She may be on to something there,' said Brandt. 'You don't seem to be interested in how I'm faring either.'

'I'm too embarrassed to ask.'

'It wasn't your fault.'

'I don't know what to say.'

'You never do.'

'Don't I?'

'Don't pretend!' he snorted. He looked like an old woman too. 'Your lodger was very concerned.'

'His name's Joachim. Why can't you call him by his name? Anyway, he's gone home now and he's taken my sister's dog with him. The lady is not amused.'

'Are you sure he took it with him? There's one loose at the moment.'

'There are other dogs, one would assume. Sometimes I think you have a very limited horizon.'

A blackbird sang. Lots of different birds sang. A moped drove along the tree-lined promenade. Mopeds were prohibited there.

'I feel like my life's a total waste,' I said.

'If your life's a total waste, then mine is too.'

'But you're a doctor. Your life can't be a total waste.'

'If you're not satisfied, then you should do something about it.'

'I wrote something yesterday, something funny. Would you like me to read it to you?'

'No, I wouldn't, thank you very much. Do something about your life.'

'I'm not in the mood for soul-searching.'

'You never are.'

'Aren't I?'

'Find some friends! Sell the house! Move!'

'Away from you?'

'You're bored.'

'I'm never bored!' Turning, I watched my sheets flapping in the wind. One time in the twilight, I had got myself tangled up in a sheet as it hung on the line, and Halland had kissed me. The thought of Halland's kiss made me dizzy. All the times he called, 'Come out, come out!' and I replied, 'In a minute!'

'Boring!' said Brandt.

'Yes, I am boring.'

'*We walk in the gloaming as we sleep!*'

'You keep saying so. And anyway, isn't that OK?'

'Did you find out who shot Halland?'

I tried to gauge his expression to see if he was making fun of me. 'I don't play at detectives.'

'Don't you want to know what happened?'

'To you? I know it was Troels. I really am sorry.'

'That's not what I meant. I was talking about Halland. About whether there are any suspects.'

'Stop it, Brandt! It's not funny!'

'It's not meant to be funny. That's not why I'm asking!'

'It's police work. I don't poke my nose in.'

He looked at me.

'I've informed them I don't want to be told anything until they know for sure.'

Deep inside his surprising blue eyes I thought I saw a gleam.

But he would get nothing from me. I wouldn't reveal what I thought about the police investigation. I would certainly not tell him that I preferred not to know anything at all.

'He's been up before the magistrate,' he said.

'Who, Troels? What on earth for? They don't think he's dangerous, surely?'

Brandt's eyes.

'They don't think he's dangerous, surely?' I repeated.

35

Also I've been, at last, in the authentic inner chambers, and I must say, they don't exist.

Robert Walser, *Jakob von Gunten*

I met the detective as I walked down the hill. He pushed up his sunglasses. 'Good thing I bumped into you!' he said. 'I've just been down at Troels's warehouse. What a mess. He had moved in there.'

'And now he'll be moving out again, won't he?'

'He certainly will!' Funder narrowed his eyes against the sun. 'I'm beginning to think that he may have been mad enough to have shot Halland.'

I thought so too, so I kept quiet.

'But there's a lot that doesn't fit.'

'Like what?' I asked politely.

'I thought you didn't want to hear anything until we knew for sure. Isn't that what you said?'

'Yes. Why did you want to speak to me now, then?'

Pushing the sunglasses back down onto his nose, he smiled and continued up the hill.

'Where did you get that tan?' I called after him.

Turning, he shrugged and pointed up at the sun.

I went to the library. Tucking the local paper under my arm, I bought a soft drink from the vending machine and went through the half-empty room to the deck. Right on the edge of the fjord, the deck resembled a café with parasols. Lasse sat at a table with a friend. Not looking at each other, they were immersed in their phones. Lasse's was blue, an old one like Halland's. 'Hi, Lasse!' I said. With a swift, seamless movement, he stuck the phone in his pocket. Smiling at me, he revealed his regular white teeth, then tossed his head back so his hair fell into place. I sat down with my back to them.

A dog came wagging its tail and sniffed at my legs under the table. 'Where did *you* come from?' I said, trying to sound friendly, but then it was gone.

I gazed across to the other side of the fjord. Everything was green. Everything had come into leaf. Soon you would be able to buy strawberries over there. We had bought some last summer. Or Halland had. He brought them home and I cheered. He said they were from the other side. They smelled delicious and tasted of the childhood you didn't enjoy but now longed for. Which place did he get them from? The water lapped between the rocks. I could hear some children further away. A happy sound.

'Lasse?' I reached back with my outstretched hand and a moment later the phone lay in my palm. I curled my fingers around it, gauging its weight. Then I threw it as far as I could. Out into the glittering fjord.

Pia Juul, born in 1962, claims her place as one of Denmark's foremost literary authors. She has published five books of poetry, two short-story collections and two novels. *The Murder of Halland* was published in Danish in 2009 and in the same year won Denmark's most important literary prize, Danske Banks Litteraturpris.

Martin Aitken holds a PhD in Linguistics. He gave up his university tenure in 2008 to listen to *The Fall* and translate literature. His works include books by Janne Teller, Peter Høeg and Jussi Adler-Olsen. He lives in rural Denmark.

Quotations in this book from works originally published in Danish, unless otherwise stated, have been translated into English by Martin Aitken. All other translations are cited in their respective bibliographic entries below.

p. 14   *The Sorrow of Belgium* by Hugo Claus, translated by Arnold J. Pomerans (Penguin Books, 1994)

p. 20   *In the Flesh* by Christa Wolf, translated from the German by John Barrett (David R. Godine Publisher, 2005)

p. 29   *Thumbprint* by Friedrich Glauser, translated from German by Mike Mitchell (Bitter Lemon Press, 2004)

p. 31   *Af en retsmediciners bekendelser* by Preben Geertinger (Munksgaard Rosinante, 1998)

p. 34   *Danmarkshistoriens hvornår skete det* by Kai Petersen (Politiken, 1960)

p. 37   *Hyrder* by Peter Seeberg (Arena, 1970)

p. 45   *Eftersøgningen og andre noveller* by Peter Seeberg (Arena, 1962)

p. 63   *Erotiske skildringer* by Emil Aarestrup (Kristian Kongstad, 1916)

p. 81   *Vilhelms Værelse* by Tove Ditlevsen (Gyldendal, 1975)

p. 88   *Natmændsfolk og Kjæltringer* by H. P. Hansen (Gyldendal, 1921–1922)

p. 96   *Paa rejse med H. C. Andersen. Dagbogsoptegnelser* by William Bloch (Gyldendal, 1942)

p. 102 *Skovveien* by B. S. Ingemann, in *Dans lyrik 1800–1873* by Christian Winther (Forlagsbureauet i København, 1873)

p. 107 *Elsie Lindtner* by Karen Michaëlis, translated from the Danish by Beatrice Marshall, first published in Danish in 1912, English translation reprinted in 2009

p. 114   *Four Plays* by Eugène Ionesco, translated from the French
          by Donald M. Allen (Grove Press, 1982)
p. 142   *Rumpole and the Brave New World* by John Mortimer.
          Unfinished manuscript. Published in *The Guardian*, 24
          January 2009
p. 146   *Jacob von Gunten* by Robert Walser, translated from the
          German by Christopher Middleton (NYRB Classics, 1999)

Typeset in Albertan.

Albertan was designed by the late Jim Rimmer of New Westminster, B.C., in 1982. He drew and cut the type in metal at the 16pt size in roman only; it was intended for use only at his Pie Tree Press. He drew the italic in 1985, designing it with a narrow fit and a very slight incline, and created a digital version. The family was completed in 2005, when Rimmer redrew the bold weight and called it Albertan Black. The letterforms of this family have an old-style character, with Rimmer's own calligraphic hand in evidence, especially in the italic.

Printed at the old Coach House on bpNichol Lane in Toronto, Ontario, on Rolland Opaque Natural paper, which was manufactured, acid-free, in Saint-Jérôme, Quebec, from 50 percent recycled paper.. This book was printed with vegetable-based ink on a 1965 Heidelberg KORD offset litho press. Its pages were folded on a Baumfolder, gathered by hand, bound on Sulby Auto-Minabinda and trimmed on a Polar single-knife cutter.

Cover design by Ingrid Paulson

Coach House Books
80 bpNichol Lane
Toronto ON M5S 3J4
Canada

416 979 2217
800 367 6360

mail@chbooks.com
www.chbooks.com